Milos and Amira

Also by Tom Milton
The Lost Summer
The Lineman
The Last Resort
The Godmother
Eden Valley
The Silver Locket
Orphans of War
Invisible Wounds
Leave of Absence
Outside the Gate
The Golden Door
Sara's Laughter
A Shower of Roses
Infamy
All the Flowers
The Admiral's Daughter
No Way to Peace

Milos and Amira

Tom Milton

NEPPERHAN PRESS, LLC
YONKERS, NY

Copyright © Tom Milton, 2021

All rights reserved. No part of this book may be reproduced or transmitted in any form or by any means, electronic or mechanical, including photocopying, recording, or by any information storage and retrieval system, without written permission from the author, except for the inclusion of brief quotations in a review.

Published by Nepperhan Press, LLC
P.O. Box 1448, Yonkers, NY 10702
nepperhan@optonline.net
nepperhan.com

PUBLISHER'S NOTE

This is a work of fiction. Names, characters, places, and incidents are the product of the author's imagination or are used fictitiously, and any resemblance to actual persons, living or dead, events, or locales is entirely coincidental.

Printed in the United States of America

Library of Congress Control Number: 2021930926

ISBN 978-1-7320634-8-8

Cover art was licensed from Publitek, Inc.

For Marie

Blessed are the peacemakers,
for they will be called children of God.
Matthew 5:9

Yonkers, 2001

Chapter 1

SINCE THE COLLEGE had cancelled classes the day after the attack on the World Trade Center, today was only the second meeting of her religion class, so Sister Maura didn't yet expect to know all her students, but in taking attendance she didn't remember ever seeing the girl who responded as Amira Hasanic, though she had marked Amira present in the first class.

"Amira, were you here last Monday?" Sister Maura asked, beginning to wonder if she was slipping. She had just turned sixty-five.

"Yes, sister," the girl said softly with a foreign accent. She was a beautiful girl, with lush dark hair and soulful dark eyes. Presumably she was eighteen, but she looked about sixteen. Of course every year the students looked younger.

"Did I say your name correctly?" Sister Maura had pronounced it "Ameera."

"Yes, sister," the girl said with lowered eyes.

When she called the name of the next student, whose name was Eduardo Hernandez, Sister Maura noticed that a boy seated two desks away from Amira was gazing at her as if he not only hadn't seen her in the first class but also hadn't seen anyone like her in his whole life. From her years of experience with students Sister Maura recognized the look—it was love at first sight. And then she suddenly realized that the reason she didn't remember seeing Amira in the first class was that then the girl was wearing a headscarf.

She could understand why Amira no longer wore the scarf. In response to the attack on September 11 there was a wave of anti-Muslim sentiment, even at the college, and the girl didn't want to draw attention to the fact that she was a Muslim. But removing the headscarf had drawn attention to the fact that she was a beautiful girl.

Continuing to take attendance, Sister Maura came to Milos Stojanovic. She recalled that in the first class he had asked her to pronounce his name "Meelos," so she said it that way now. "Milos?"

"I'm here, sister." This was the boy who had gazed at Amira as if he was in love with her. He had sweet blue eyes and curly fair hair. A silver cross on a silver chain around his neck hung visibly outside of his shirt. She had noticed the cross in the first class because although it wasn't unusual for a girl to wear a cross outside of her shirt, it was unusual for a boy. From an image in her memory she recognized it as some type of Orthodox cross.

"Did I say your name correctly?"

"Yes, sister," the boy said, still in a daze.

Sister Maura marked him present. It occurred to her that since the last names of the girl and the boy had the same ending they could be from the same country, or from a region with the same language. She guessed it was in former Yugoslavia.

As she called out the remaining names she noticed that Milos just couldn't take his eyes off Amira, who acted as if she was completely unaware of him.

"All right," Sister Maura said after finishing attendance. "We missed a class last Wednesday, so we're a little behind schedule. But I don't want to move ahead without talking about what happened last Tuesday."

Her students waited trustingly for her to continue.

"We know of two students who were lost in the towers, and we know of several who found their way to safety by the grace of God. If any of you lost family members or friends, my heart goes out to you, and my prayers are with you."

She didn't expect any of them to speak up, and no one did, though at least some of them must have heard their parents talking about people they knew who had perished in the towers.

"So let's talk about how we feel."

A boy raised his hand.

"Yes. You are?"

"Steve," he said. "I feel angry."

"I understand. How many of you feel angry?"

About half of the twenty students raised their hands. She noticed that neither Amira nor Milos was among them.

"It's okay to feel angry. But it's not okay to act on that feeling."

"I think we should kill the people who did it," Steve said.

"The people who did it died in the attack," Sister Maura pointed out.

"Then we should kill the people who planned it."

"Who are they?"

"Muslims."

"They may have been Muslims, but they didn't do it because of their religion."

"Then why did they do it?"

"Why do you think?"

After a silence a girl raised her hand.

"Yes. You are?"

"Tanya. I think they did it because they were angry at us."

"I think you're right," Sister Maura said. "And I think they acted on that feeling. They did what we should not do."

"Then what *should* we do?" Steve asked.

"We should understand what made them angry, and we should do something about that."

"Do you know what made them angry?" another girl asked.

"What makes you angry?"

The girl shrugged. "Being treated like shit."

"I understand. How many of you feel angry when you're treated like shit?"

All of the students raised their hands.

"So we understand what made them angry," Sister Maura said, "and we know what we should do about it."

"You mean," Steve said doubtfully, "we should stop treating them like shit?"

"Yeah, that would be a start."

"But it wouldn't be enough," Milos said, coming out of nowhere. "It's not enough to stop treating people badly. We should love them."

"Love Muslims?" Steve said, making a face.

"They're children of God."

"They are," Sister Maura agreed. "Whatever our religion, we're children of God."

"The men who flew those planes into the towers," Milos said, "were filled with hate, so there was no room in their hearts for love. If they'd had any love in their hearts, they never would have done it. So it wasn't their religion that made them attack us, it was their hate."

She waited for other students to respond to this statement, but they sat there in silence, some of them looking as if they vaguely understood what Milos had said and others looking as if they wondered where he had come from. She noticed that Amira was gazing at Milos as if she perfectly understood what he had said.

Instead of rushing to leave when the class was over, Milos lingered until the girl got up and headed out. He followed her, trying not to be obvious. The hallway was thronged with students because it was the fifteen-minute interval between classes. Some students were heading for the bathrooms, others for the cafeteria, others for the rooms where they had their next classes, and others for home. He hoped that the girl wasn't heading for home.

He followed her past the room where he had his next class and all the way to the end of the hallway, where she went into a classroom. He noted the room number, and then he walked back to where the courses with their room numbers were posted on a bulletin board. It took him a while, but he finally found the room number with the course that met at this time. It was the introductory course in sociology. It ran until one, as his class did, so he would have a chance to meet her, provided that her instructor didn't let the class out early.

For the next hour and twenty minutes he sat in his biology class thinking about her. He liked girls, and girls liked him, but he had never been in love before. He had started high school a year after arriving with his family from Bosnia, and until his junior year he spoke English so badly, with such a heavy accent, that most people had trouble understanding him. But the girls hadn't seemed to mind. They treated him as if he was cute and exotic, and they helped him with his English. The boys mostly tolerated him.

It was one of those girls who had talked him into going to St. Catherine, assuring him that even though it was a Catholic college they welcomed people of all faiths, and they were by far the most affordable private college in the region. Above all, they offered the program he wanted to pursue, so he had applied and been accepted and given enough financial aid to cover all of his tuition. Now he was in his second week of classes, grateful to his advisor for suggesting the religion course.

While the professor talked about the chemistry of life, Milos closed his eyes and saw the girl's face and was carried away in yearning. He felt as if he had been lifted bodily into the air, where he floated toward her.

Luckily, his professor let the class out a few minutes early, and Milos hurried down the hallway toward the classroom that the girl had gone into. Taking a peek, he ascertained that the class was still in session, so he stepped back and waited for her, intending to engage her in a conversation but not knowing what he would say.

When the students finally started coming out he edged forward, and when she emerged he moved a little into her path, enough to make her stop.

"I think you're in my religion class," he managed to say, stating an undeniable fact.

"I am," she admitted, gazing at him with those dark eyes.

In the pause that followed their verbal exchange something miraculous flowed between them that taught him all he needed to know about the chemistry of life.

"Do you have another class now?" he asked, hoping she didn't.

"No. I don't. But I have to go to work now."

"How do you get there?"

"I take the bus."

"So you're going to the bus stop?"

"I'm going there right now."

"Well, I'm going to the bus stop too. Can I go there with you?" She nodded. "Sure."

"I'm Milos," he said as they headed down the hallway.

"I'm Amira," she said shyly. "I liked what you said about the terrorists. I mean about how it wasn't their religion that made them attack us, it was their hate."

"I know what people do when they're filled with hate. My family came to America to get away from it."

"Mine did too."

"When did you come here?"

"Five years ago."

"That's when we came here," he said. He was about to ask her where she came from, but an instinct made him change the subject. "What's your major?"

"Social work. What's yours?"

"Physical therapy."

"So we both have to get graduate degrees."

"Yeah, we'll be here for six years."

"Why did you take the religion class?"

"My advisor suggested it."

"Mine did too."

They left Wagner Hall and started walking along the path that led to North Broadway, where the Bee-Line buses ran. Not knowing where else to go with the conversation, Milos asked: "Which bus do you take?"

"The number one."

"Where do you work?"

"At a deli on McLean Avenue."

"Do you work every day?"

"Yeah. Where do you work?"

"At the A&P on Nepperhan Avenue."

"What bus do you take?"

"The number nine."

They walked in silence for a while as if they had run out of things to say.

Then Milos asked: "Did you miss the first class in religion?"

"No. I was there."

"I don't remember seeing you."

"Well, I was there." She acted as if she was going to explain why he didn't remember seeing her, but instead she said: "I like Sister Maura."

"I do too. I like the way she gets the students into discussions."

"My sociology professor doesn't do that. She just lectures."

"Lectures can be boring."

"Yeah. They can."

They were now at the bus stop. The bus she was taking, the Bee-Line number one, stopped on this side of North Broadway and ran south to downtown Yonkers. The bus he was taking, the number nine, stopped on the other side of the street and ran north to Executive Boulevard. According to the schedule her bus would arrive seven minutes before his, so he waited with her on this side until it came, and then he crossed the street.

He didn't have to wait long, and he took a seat near the front, next to a window, where he could look at the scenery. The bus turned at Executive Boulevard and headed east and passed some office buildings, a restaurant, and a gas station, and then it wound downhill into the valley carved by the Saw Mill River. Compared with the Bosna River, which flowed through Zenica, the Saw Mill River wasn't much, and compared with the mountains around Zenica, the hills of Yonkers weren't much. He closed his eyes and pictured Zenica, missing it but accepting the fact that he would never see it again.

In retrospect, his Uncle Goran had been smart to leave Zenica in the late 1980s. He had seen the trouble coming in Yugoslavia, and he had tried to talk Milos's father into going with him. But Milos's mother didn't want to leave Zenica, where she had spent her entire life, so his father had bought his uncle's share of the machine shop that they owned jointly, and Uncle Goran had taken his family to America.

When the war started, his family tried not to get involved in it. Zenica was a mixture of Bosniaks, Croats, and Serbs who as far as Milos knew got along fine together. They all spoke the same language, they all went to the same school, and they all went to the same stadium for football games. The only apparent differences between them were that Bosniaks were Muslim, Croats were Catholic, and Serbs were Orthodox. But those differences meant nothing to boys whose main interest in life was sports.

It came as a surprise when Milos learned that as a Serb he was outnumbered in the region by Bosniaks, and as the war intensified he encountered hostility from people who had been his friends and neighbors. According to his father, the Bosniaks were driving the Serbs out of the city. And Bosniak refugees from other parts of the war-torn country were pouring into Zenica, increasing their majority.

His father, hoping that the war would end and things would return to normal, stuck it out until the family received two blows in the same week. The first blow was a fire that destroyed the machine shop, believed to be arson. His grandmother, who had reasons for hating the Croats, blamed the Croats. His father, who resented the Bosniaks for taking over the city, blamed the Bosniaks. His mother still didn't want to leave, but she was convinced by the second blow, the death of her only brother, believed to be an execution. For that his grandmother blamed the Croats, while his father blamed the Bosniaks. His mother didn't blame anyone, and she even asked God to forgive whoever had killed her brother.

Having lost everything in the war, his family came to Yonkers and moved into Uncle Goran's house on Woodland Avenue. It was a two-family house, and Milos's family lived upstairs where there was more room. They needed more room because there were six of them: his grandmother, his father, his mother, himself, and his two sisters, who were fourteen and sixteen. There were only four in Uncle Goran's family.

Milos got off at Odell Avenue. The A&P was right there, so he only had to walk across the parking lot. As usual, he was about ten minutes early for his shift, which began at two. He went into the room where the employees hung out and chatted for a while with Marta, a Dominican girl who also worked from two to six, and then after clipping on his identification badge he went to take his position at the number seven checkout counter.

As he stood there his mind was elsewhere, but luckily he didn't have to think much in this job because most of the time he was only running the barcode by the sensing device. In his memory he walked with Amira to the bus stop, and in his imagination he got on the bus with her and rode with her to downtown Yonkers.

Amira gazed out the window at St. John's Hospital, which the bus had stopped in front of. She had gone there once to visit her Aunt Malika, who was in a room on the eighth floor recovering from surgery. That was only a few months after her family arrived in America, and she didn't understood much English. She was afraid of losing her aunt, as she had lost her mother.

As the bus moved forward her thoughts returned again to the boy she had met in religion class. He was such a nice boy, and he was cute. Whatever happened, she could count on seeing him in the classroom twice a week until the end of the semester.

"Milos, Milos," she whispered to the window. She had never known anyone by that name, so it had no associations for her. The way he pronounced it, she knew it wasn't American, and even if his name had been Mike she would have known he wasn't born in America. And he had talked about his family coming to America to get away from all that hate.

Staring out the window, she remembered what the war had done to her family. After being expelled from Srebrenica, which was supposed to be protected by the UN but was captured by the Serbs after a siege, her father made sure that she and her mother were on a bus that would take them to Bosniak-controlled territory before he and her brother Kashir joined the men who were trying to escape across the countryside.

The bus was filled with women and children, but a few men were hidden on board. It had left Potoćari and was on the road to Kladanj when it was stopped by Serb soldiers. The soldiers searched the bus and found the men and made them get off. They also selected a few women to get off, including her mother. Screaming, Amira tried to go with her mother, but two strong women held her back, gripping her wrists with hands like clamps. They saved her from being raped and killed like her mother, and she knew she should be grateful to them. But she still felt guilty about not sharing her mother's fate.

Her father and brother were among the few men who made it to safety. Thousands of men in the column of refugees were caught and systematically executed at Sandići, Karvica, Konjhević, Polje, Lolići, Tišča, Petkovići, Kozluk, and other places. Amira knew the names by heart, having heard her father recite them in a litany of mourning.

"If they'd had any love in their hearts," she heard Milos say, "they never would have done it."

"In the name of God, the Lord of Mercy," she said silently, reciting a prayer she had learned from her mother. "Look with compassion on the whole human family. Take away the teachings of arrogance, divisions, and hatreds that have infected our hearts. Break down the walls that separate us. Reunite us in the bonds of love. And help us in our struggles and confusions to accomplish your purposes on earth, so that all nations and races may serve you in justice, harmony, and peace."

She got off at the corner of South Broadway and McLean Avenue. She walked along McLean toward the deli where she and her father worked. The deli was owned by her Uncle Ahmed, who had come to America more than ten years ago. The deli served sandwiches and American dishes like beef stew, but it also had things like *dolmades* that you would find in a Greek deli. People might have thought her family was Greek, except that Aunt Malika, who worked at the counter from eight in the morning until two in the afternoon, wore a headscarf.

Amira's father worked in the kitchen, where knowing English wasn't necessary. He had owned a restaurant in Srebrenica, and knowing how to cook made him valuable to Uncle Ahmed, who no longer had to worry about the kitchen and could now worry about other things. Amira worked at the counter, relieving Aunt Malika at two and remaining there until the deli closed at seven. Since the peak hours were at breakfast and lunch, Amira wasn't always busy, so she had time between serving customers to study for her courses.

When she walked into the deli Amira wasn't wearing her headscarf, which she had put into her backpack shortly after leaving home that morning. She hadn't worn it on the street since the day after the attack on the World Trade Center, when a guy on South Broadway had snarled at her: "You dirty Muslim. You deserve to die."

"Where's your headscarf?" Aunt Malika asked her.

"It's in my backpack," Amira said.

"It doesn't belong in your backpack, it belongs on your head."

"I'm afraid to wear it. People threaten me."

Aunt Malika frowned. "So you're renouncing your religion because people threaten you?"

"I'm not renouncing my religion. And anyway, there's nothing in the Quran that says women have to wear headscarves."

"You're telling me what's in the Quran?"

"No. I'm telling you what's *not* in the Quran."

"Well, put on your headscarf. If you're going to work here, you're not going to flaunt your hair to the customers."

"I'm not flaunting my hair."

"You are if you don't cover it."

Without further argument Amira took her headscarf out of her backpack and put it on.

"That's better," Aunt Malika said, patting her shoulder. "Be a good girl, so your mother in heaven will be proud of you."

She understood why her aunt invoked her mother to keep her in line: it always worked.

"How's college?"

"It's fine."

"Fine? Can you be more specific?"

"I have good professors, and I like my courses."

"What courses did you have today?"

"Religion and sociology."

"Why are you taking a course on religion?"

"To learn about other religions."

"What religions does the course cover?"

"Judaism, Christianity, and Islam."

"Who's teaching it?"

"Sister Maura."

"If she's a nun, she'll have a bias against Islam."

"No, I don't think she will," Amira said. "Today we talked about the attack, and when a boy blamed Muslims for it and talked about killing us, she told him that whatever our religion, we're children of God."

"She doesn't sound like a typical Catholic."

"She's nice. I like her."

"Well, I still have reservations about your going to a Catholic college, but there aren't any Muslim colleges."

"I don't think it matters. I think what matters is getting a good education."

"I agree. And I'm sure your mother would agree."

At that moment Uncle Ahmed came in through the front door, followed by a man in uniform with a Budweiser logo on the shirt. Though consuming alcohol was against his religion, Uncle Ahmed made a lot of money selling beer. In fact, he had a whole refrigerated case filled with beer, including Corona, Modelo, and Presidente for the Latino customers.

"Hi, princess," he said to Amira. That was the meaning of her name, and he always said it with affection. Unlike her father, he was outgoing and friendly. Even among his family he often acted like an American.

"Hi, Uncle Ahmed," she said, smiling.

"We have a beer delivery," he said as if it was a major event. He led the man in uniform back to the case where they displayed the beer.

"Well, I'm going home," Aunt Malika said.

"I'll be home at five," Uncle Ahmed told her. "Tarik and Amira will lock up."

When her aunt had gone Amira positioned herself behind the counter. From there she could see her father in the kitchen, standing at the stove in his white attire. She caught his eye and waved to him. He raised the utensil in his hand, acknowledging her, and though he didn't smile, there was a glimmer in his eyes that made her feel she was his treasure.

Her first customer was a Latina. So many of their customers were Latinos that Amira and Aunt Malika had learned enough

Spanish to communicate with them. This woman's name was Rosa, and like a lot of other Mexicans in the neighborhood she was from Puebla. She was in her early twenties, with two young children.

In a shopping basket Rosa collected the items she needed and brought them to the counter, saying: *"Hola, Amira. Cómo estás?"*

"Muy bien, y tú?"

"Bien, gracias a Dios."

Amira rang up the items, using the simple machine that Uncle Ahmed insisted was much better than any computer. The store was cash only, but that didn't deter their customers, few of whom had credit cards or bank accounts. She put the items into a plastic bag while Rosa found the money in her handbag. Rosa cleaned houses, and she must have come here directly from work. Her husband did construction. They lived on South Broadway in an apartment where Rosa's mother would be babysitting the children.

As she watched the woman leave the store Amira admired her. She knew how hard it was to leave your country, even when you had no choice. But when you had a choice, it must be harder because in that situation you voluntarily gave things up.

When Uncle Ahmed had finished with the beer distributor he sat down at a narrow desk behind the counter and reviewed his accounts. He had wanted Amira to major in accounting, but she didn't like working with numbers. She liked working with people. And she had finally convinced her uncle, her aunt, and even her father that being a social worker was a respectable profession. Of course, they all expected her to get married and have children.

The thought of being married and having children stirred her nascent feelings about Milos. She knew that her heart was racing way ahead of things, but she could already imagine him as her husband and as the father of her children.

"Silly girl," she told herself. "You hardly know him."

For the rest of the afternoon there was a trickle of customers, and then around five-thirty it got busy as a lot of people came home from work. A lot of them bought the hot dishes that her father had cooked, and they ran out of meatballs.

By then Uncle Ahmed had gone home, and her father was cleaning up the kitchen.

At seven, after locking the front door, she began to carry the salads and other cold dishes into the kitchen, where she put them into the refrigerator. The green salad wouldn't be good the next day, so she disposed of it, but the tuna and chicken and egg salads would still be good.

She was carrying the leftover beef stew into the kitchen when she heard a noise at the front window. She turned and saw a motion across the pane.

When she had put the stew into the refrigerator she went out to see what had happened.

Across the front window someone had sprayed: "Muslims, go home."

She was staring at the message in distress when her father joined her on the sidewalk.

"*Dovraga*," he moaned. "I thought we left the hate behind us."

"It's because of the attack," she said, not wanting to believe there was more to it.

"It must have been there all along," her father murmured. "The attack only brought it out."

"Well, I don't think it was anyone from our neighborhood."

"I hope it wasn't. But I don't know." Her father left her, went inside, and then came back with a scraper he used to clean the grill. And he began to scrape at the message.

"Can I help?" she asked.

"No, I'll take care of this. Go and finish putting the food away."

She went and did what her father had asked. She put all the food away except for the chicken and rice and vegetables that they would take home for dinner. By the time she was ready to go her father had finished scraping the message off the window.

Amira held the containers of food while her father locked the door. As usual the money from the register was in her backpack. Later that evening she would give it to Aunt Malika, who would open the store in the morning.

After double checking to make sure the door was locked, her father took the containers from her and they headed home.

As they walked to Cornell Avenue, where they lived on the lower floor of Uncle Ahmed's two-family house, she gently took her father's arm, imagining the painful memories that the message on the window had aroused in him.

As she did every evening, Sister Maura went to the college chapel to pray. She had a list of people she prayed for that had gotten longer over the years. It included members of her family, some of them alive and some of them no longer on this earth. It included colleagues and people in positions of leadership. And of course it included her students.

Last spring she had completed forty years of teaching at the college. In preparing for an event to honor her service she had calculated that she must have had about eight thousand students during her years as a teacher. Of course, she didn't remember them all, and she had no idea how many of them remembered her. But some of them she would never forget. At the top of that list was Teri Ryan, the girl who in singing "I know that my redeemer liveth" declared her faith without any questions, doubts, or reservations. Whether she was singing or playing basketball or working to end the Vietnam War, she did it with all her heart and all her mind and all her soul. Teri would always have a special place in Sister Maura's prayers.

She had finished the list when she thought of the boy and girl in her religion class. From the way the boy gazed at the girl upon seeing her for the first time, and the way the girl gazed at the boy upon hearing him say it wasn't enough to stop treating people badly, we should love them, Sister Maura believed they had fallen in love. She didn't know enough about them to know what the problem would be, but her instincts told her there would be a problem. So she ended by praying for Milos and Amira.

Chapter 2

IT WAS ONLY a short walk from the A&P to his Uncle Goran's house on Woodland Avenue, so Milos was home by ten after six. In front of the house was his cousin Bojan's black pickup truck, which always looked brand new. Bojan worked as a mechanic in the auto repair shop on Saw Mill River Road that Uncle Goran had established a few years after coming to America. It was a good business, and it supported the extended family, providing a job for Milos's father, who was now a junior partner. Bojan's mother had wanted him to go to college, but Bojan wanted to pursue his passion for cars and trucks. He lived for them, and he loved them more than anything in the world, especially his truck.

As he walked around it Milos noticed a sticker on the rear bumper that hadn't been there a week ago. It said: "Muslims, go home." That was typical of Bojan, who hated immigrants. He always referred to Latinos as "illegals," conveniently ignoring the fact that he himself was an immigrant who had come to this country only ten years ago.

Wishing his cousin would make more room in his heart for love, Milos went into the house and climbed the stairs and let himself into the apartment where his family lived. His father and mother weren't home from work, but he found his grandmother in the kitchen preparing dinner. She was a bony woman with tightly bound white hair and hard blue eyes.

"Dobro veče," Baka said with her usual formality. Though she had learned some English from shopping and watching television, she always spoke Serbian.

"Dobro veče," Milos replied. "What's for dinner?"

"Roast chicken."

"Mm. It smells good."

"I got it on sale from the A&P."

She could have given him a list of things to bring home from work, but she preferred to do the shopping herself. He understood because she was home alone all day, and she had only one Serb friend in the neighborhood.

"Are the girls home?"

"They're in their room."

He knew better than to disturb Jovana and Tijana. They would be talking privately, changing the subject from hair to boys, from clothes to boys, from friends to boys, and from music to boys. On one wall of their room was a poster of Enrique Iglesias, who they agreed was the sexiest guy in the whole world.

"How's college?" Baka asked after taking a peek into the oven.

"It's fine," he said, bracing himself.

"I still don't think you should go to a Catholic college." Baka had argued passionately against his going to St. Catherine, citing the atrocities committed by the Catholic Croats during World War II when a fascist government aligned with the Nazis had rounded up Serbs as well as Jews and herded them into concentration camps and systematically exterminated them. Baka had firsthand knowledge of the genocide, having spent two years as a preteen girl in Jasenovac, the most notorious of the camps. She had watched as her father and brothers were taken away to be executed. She had watched as her mother died of malnutrition. She had been kept alive only because the Croat soldiers had designs on her as soon as she was old enough to give them pleasure. By the grace of God, she was physically intact when the war ended.

"It's a good college," Milos argued.

"It can't be good. It's a Catholic college."

"I know what they did to your family, but they didn't do it because of their religion."

"Then why did they do it?"

"They did it because Croats and Serbs hate each other."

"And why do they hate each other?"

"I don't know. I don't understand why people hate each other. But I think it starts when one group treats another group badly."

"That *is* how it started. The Croats treated us badly."

"Well, maybe," he suggested, "they were getting even with us for treating them badly."

"No. The Croats started it."

"If that's how you feel, then how are you ever going to stop hating Croats?"

"I never am. I don't want to stop hating them."

"I thought we came here to get away from all that hate."

"We came here because we had nothing left there," Baka told him. "The Croats destroyed your father's business. And they killed my only son."

"Dad says the Bosniaks did it."

"The Croats and the Bosniaks ganged up against us. But it was the Croats who wanted to get rid of us. They always wanted to get rid of us."

"Even if that's true, the sisters who run the college aren't Croats. They're Irish and Italian."

"They're still Catholics," Baka snapped, "and Catholics are fascists."

Milos paused, debating whether to continue the argument. He had almost decided to retreat to his room when his mother came home. She worked as a nanny for a rich family in Irvington who had two small children. They paid her ten dollars an hour and gave her money to take the bus. It was the best job his mother could get until she learned more English.

After giving him a tender kiss his mother asked him to call the girls and ask them to set the table for dinner. His mother did everything possible to make sure they ate dinner together as a family, as they had in Zenica

There had been a separate dining room in this apartment, but since they needed four bedrooms they had converted it to a bedroom, so the dining table was in the living room, leaving less space for a sitting area. Still, there was enough room for all of them to gather in the living room, even if the children had to sit on the carpet, so if there was something on television that they all wanted to watch they could all gather there.

But most of the time they watched television separately because they liked different things. His mother and father liked the news, which helped them learn English. His sisters liked the pop music channels. Milos liked football, or soccer as they called it here. And his grandmother liked soap operas, which she more or less followed without understanding what the people were saying. If the children were around, she would ask them to translate.

Milos had gone to the door of their room and called his sisters when his father came home. As usual his father headed for the bathroom, where he took a quick shower and changed into clean clothes. By the time his father emerged from the bathroom the table was set and his mother had put food on the table.

They always sat in the same places, with his father at the head of the table, his mother at the foot, his sisters on one side, and he and his grandmother on the other side.

Before they started passing the food around, his mother bowed her head and said grace: *"Bože, zahvaljujemo ti na svemu što si nam dao.* We thank you for our safety, our home, our health, our jobs, and our schools. We thank you for bringing us to America, where we can live in peace and look forward to a better future."

"Amen," they all said.

His father carved the chicken while they passed the bowls of potatoes and carrots. Milos and his father liked the legs and thighs, while the women liked the slices of breast, so they all had enough of what they liked. Tijana tried to get away without taking any carrots, but his mother insisted that she take some, saying: "They're good for your eyes."

While they were eating, his father said: "I think America is going to war."

"War?" his mother said as if the word frightened her.

"The attack on the World Trade Center was like the attack on Pearl Harbor, and I think America will go to war against the people who did it."

"The people who did it died in the attack," Milos told him.

"Those people died," his father agreed. "But the people who planned it are still alive, and America will go after them."

"Go after who?" his mother asked.

"Muslims," his father said.

"I hope you're not saying that America will go to war against Muslims."

"That's what I'm saying. And it's about time. America has been letting Muslims get away with murder."

"There are a billion and a half Muslims in the world," Milos pointed out.

"There are, and they all hate America."

"They don't all hate America."

"If they didn't, then why did they attack us?"

"The people who flew the planes into the towers hated us, and the people who planned the attack hate us, but that doesn't mean all Muslims hate us."

"Well, we've been at war with Muslims since they started their religion. In fact, their religion is based on *jihad*, which means war against non-Muslims."

"From the course I'm taking," Milos said, "I'm going to learn what *jihad* means. And I bet it doesn't mean what you say."

"You'll lose that bet," his father said.

"It doesn't make sense for a religion to be about war. Religions are about love."

"Our religion is about love," his grandmother said. "But the Catholic religion is about war. Catholics are fascists."

Ignoring her, Milos asked his father: "If we go to war against Muslims, who will we go after first?"

"We'll go after al-Qaeda, who planned the attack."

"Where are they?"

"They're hiding in Afghanistan."

"How do you know?"

"I heard it on the news."

"So you think we'll go to war against Afghanistan?"

"I think we will."

"But that's stupid. That's what the terrorists want us to do."

"Oh, now you're an expert on terrorism. Are you taking a course on that too?"

"You don't have to be an expert on terrorism to understand that the whole purpose of their attack was to make us retaliate."

"Why would they want us to retaliate?"

"To start a war against Muslims."

"But that's what *we* want—a war against Muslims."

"It's not what *I* want. And it's not what the American people want."

"It *is* what they want. The American people want revenge."

"So how many Americans do you personally know?" Milos asked, challenging his father.

"I know what they want," his father insisted.

"Well, I don't believe they want revenge."

"That's because you're naïve about people, you and your mother."

"I'm not naïve," his mother said. "I just like to think there's more good than bad in people."

"I don't know where you got that idea," his grandmother said.

"I know where she didn't get it from," Milos muttered.

"What was that?"

"Nothing."

"I agree with Mom," Jovana said. "I think there's more good than bad in people."

"I do too," Tijana said, supporting her older sister.

"You're both too young to know anything," his father said.

Neither of them argued, evidently having gone as far as they dared against their father.

"I thought we came here to get away from all that hate," his mother said.

"We did," his father said. "But the hate came with us."

"The hate didn't come with us," Milos argued. "It was already here in America."

"So we didn't get away from it."

"But we should help America learn from our experience."

"What did we learn from our experience?"

"We learned that if someone hates you, you shouldn't hate them back."

"That's what Jesus taught us," his mother said.

"Jesus never had to deal with Muslims," his father said.

"If we asked Him what to do in this situation, I know what

He'd tell us to do. He'd tell us to turn the other cheek."

"You mean so they can attack us again?"

"We have to defend ourselves from attack," Milos admitted. "But we can do that without attacking them. We only have to tighten security."

"That's not enough. You know what Americans say? They say the best defense is a good offense."

"I don't think it is. A good offense in football won't stop the other team from scoring a goal."

"It'll keep them occupied."

"But if you spread your defense, they could slip through it."

"This isn't football," his father reminded him.

He knew he wouldn't have the last word with his father, so he stopped arguing as he had with his grandmother. Though she was his mother's mother, Baka and his mother were very different while Baka and his father were very alike. The difference was that Baka hated Catholics and his father hated Muslims.

In his room, with the door closed so that he could study without being disturbed, Milos recalled his conversations in the kitchen and at the dinner table. After all they had suffered he understood why his grandmother hated Catholics and why his father hated Muslims. But he believed what Sister Maura had said in class: it was okay to feel anger, but it wasn't okay to act on that feeling. And in his opinion talking the way his grandmother and his father talked wasn't okay because words could lead to actions.

He wished he could change how they felt, but he didn't see how. Their feelings were based on what had happened to them, and he couldn't change that any more than he could change what had happened to him in Zenica.

At the time he was thirteen, and his main interest in life was sports. He went to the games of the local football club, Celik Zenica, as often as he could talk his father into taking him. In fact, his last happy memory of Zenica was in 1995 when their team won the league championship. It also won the championship in 1996 and 1997, but by then he was living in Yonkers, and it was hard to get results of the games.

Milos not only went to football games, but he also played almost every day with his friends. They played on the school field or on a vacant lot in the neighborhood. There were usually about twenty of them, and the two goalkeepers would act as captains, selecting players so that the teams would be as evenly matched as possible. If there were an odd number of players, they would rotate the players so that everyone had an equal chance to play.

The boys were a mixture of Bosniaks, Croats, and Serbs, but their ethnic group didn't matter. All that mattered were their abilities in playing football.

Things changed when the war started. Milos became aware of the fact that one of the goalkeepers was Bosniak and the other was Croat, and that there were only a few Serbs among the players.

One afternoon he stood among them while the goalkeepers selected the teams. He was usually among the first players selected, but for some reason the goalkeepers ignored him. They also ignored a boy named Vasilije, a talented forward.

When they were the only players left, the Croat goalkeeper said: "That's it."

"What do you mean?" Milos objected.

"We have enough players. We don't need you."

"So are we going to be substitutes?" Vasilije asked.

"We don't need substitutes," the Bosniak goalkeeper said.

"I don't understand," Milos said. "We've been playing football together for years."

"Well, things have changed," the Croat goalkeeper said.

Vasilije confronted the goalkeeper, asking: "Are you saying you don't want us to play with you because we're Serbs?"

"We're saying we don't need you."

"Oh, that's a load of shit. Without us you only have eighteen players."

"Eighteen players are enough."

"Twenty are better. Why don't you admit it?"

"Admit what?"

"That you don't want us to play with you because we're Serbs."

At that point a Bosniak boy interjected: "Do you guys have any idea what your people are doing to our people?"

"Whatever they're doing," Vasilije said, "we're not doing it. We're your friends."

"You're killing our men and raping our women."

"We haven't killed anyone, and we haven't raped anyone."

"Maybe you haven't, but your people have."

"If they have," Milos said, "we're sorry for it. But we haven't done anything to you. We've known each other all our lives, and we never had problems before."

"We have problems now," the Bosniak goalkeeper said.

"They're not our problems," Vasilije said. "They're the problems of old people who can't forget the past."

"We don't have to hate each other," Milos said, "just because old people hate each other."

"I don't hate you as a person," the Croat goalkeeper said. "I just hate Serbs."

"If you hate them, it's because your parents hate them."

"My parents have reasons for hating them."

"But you don't have reasons for hating us. What have Serbs ever done to you?"

The Croat goalkeeper stopped to think.

"You see?" Vasilije said. "You can't think of anything we ever did to you."

"Well, even if I can't, do you expect me to go home and tell my parents I played football today with Serbs?"

"You've been playing football with us for years."

"But things have changed."

"We haven't changed," Milos insisted. "We're the same people we were before."

"Maybe we are," the Bosniak goalkeeper said. "But we can't pretend things haven't changed. They *have* changed. And we don't want you to play with us anymore."

As they walked away Vasilije said: "I hate them."

"Don't hate them. If you do, it'll never end."

"But how are we going to play football now? There're only two of us."

"We can play together. We can practice our kicks and work on our moves. So when they let us play with them again, we'll be in shape."

"You think they'll let us play with them again?"

"I think they will. We're all friends."

When Milos got home he didn't tell his parents what had happened. He didn't want to give them evidence to support their belief that Bosniaks and Croats were ganging up on Serbs. And he certainly didn't want to provoke his father into doing anything about it.

For the next few weeks Milos and Vasilije got together after school and went to the park on the Bosna River, where they practiced their kicks and worked on their moves. It wasn't like playing a game with eighteen other boys, but it was better than not playing at all. They kept hoping that the other boys would let them play with them again, but the Bosniaks and Croats didn't show any signs of relenting. They didn't even speak to them at school.

One evening Milos and Vasilije were walking along the river, going home after playing in the park, when they were stopped by two men in uniform. It was dusk, and the men appeared like shadows out of nowhere.

"What are you doing here?" the tall one demanded.

"We're walking home," Milos said respectfully.

"Where do you live?"

Milos's parents had often warned him not to tell strangers where he lived, so he evaded the question, saying: "Across town."

"Where exactly?"

"We don't have to tell you," Vasilije said.

"You don't, uh. I'm going to count to ten, and if you haven't told us where you live—" The man made a gesture across his throat as if he was slitting it.

Milos told him the neighborhood without giving the exact address.

"That's a Serb neighborhood," the stocky man said.

It actually wasn't. They had neighbors who were Bosniaks, Croats, and even Montenegrins. But he didn't argue.

"What are your names?" the tall man asked.

They only gave their first names.

The stocky man nodded as if he might have guessed. "Those are Serb names."

"So you're Serbs?" the tall man said.

By now Milos couldn't deny it. "Yes. We're Serbs. But we're not your enemies."

"We decide who our enemies are, and you're our enemies."

"We never did anything to you," Vasilije said.

"Do you know what's happening in our country now?"

"Yeah. We're having a war."

"That's right. And you know what? We should kill you just for being Serbs. Because that's what the Serbs are doing to us."

"That would be cowardly," Vasilije said. "We're only thirteen years old."

"It would be wrong," Milos said. "Killing is a sin."

"Well, tell that to your people. They're killing boys your age, and they're raping girls your age. So why shouldn't we kill you?"

"Because two wrongs don't make a right," Milos said.

"That's a good reason," the tall man admitted, looking at Milos. "What do you have there?"

"A ball," Milos said.

"Let me see it."

Milos hesitated. The ball was a birthday present from his parents, which they had scraped up money to buy.

"If I tell you to do something, you better do it."

Milos handed over the ball.

The man inspected the ball, saying: "It's a nice ball. My kid could use it."

"Please give it back. It was a present from my parents."

"They can buy you another ball. It's a small price to pay for your life."

"You have no right to take it," Milos said.

"You're a big bully," Vasilije said.

The tall man smiled. "I have to admit, you kids have balls. Or else you don't realize that we could kill you on the spot and throw your bodies into the river, and no one would ever know what happened to you."

"I don't see any reason why we shouldn't kill them," the stocky man said.

"I do," the tall man said. "Two wrongs don't make a right."

The stocky man looked at him as if he was crazy, and then they both laughed.

"You better run on home," the tall man said. "Your parents will be worried about you."

"Come on," Milos said, starting to walk.

Vasilije went along with him.

After going only a short distance they glanced back to see if the men were following them, but the men had vanished, and Milos might have wondered if he had imagined the whole thing, except that he no longer had his ball.

Vasilije said: "I hate them. Now we don't even have a ball to play with."

"We can get another ball," Milos said, not knowing where they would get the money. But right now his biggest worry was what to tell his parents when he arrived home without the ball. If he told them the truth, it would all come out.

The question arose the next morning when his father went to get his coat out of the front closet, where Milos usually kept the ball.

"Where's your ball?" his father asked, coming into the kitchen.

Milos was at the table eating breakfast, dressed for school. "My ball?"

"Your ball. Where is it?"

He considered telling his father that the ball was in his room, but even if he got away with it, sooner or later he would have to tell his father what had happened. And it wasn't as if he had done something wrong. "I lost it."

"How did you lose it?"

"Someone took it from me."

"Who took it?"

"A soldier. He said if I didn't hand it over, he'd kill me."

"Where did this happen?"

"By the river. Vasilije and I were walking home, and two men in uniform stopped us."

"Were they Bosniaks?"

"I don't know. They weren't Serbs."

"Of course they weren't Serbs," his father said. "They were either Bosniaks or Croats. But since there are more Bosniaks, they were probably Bosniaks."

"I'm sorry," Milos said, feeling responsible.

"You don't have anything to be sorry for. But I do."

"What are you sorry for?"

"I'm sorry I didn't go to America with your Uncle Goran. I'm sorry I didn't get your mother and you and your sisters out of here."

"So are we going to America now?"

"It's harder now. We should have gone then."

"Well, I don't need a ball," Milos said. "I can live without it."

"That's not the point," his father said gloomily. "They took your ball, so it won't be long before they take our house."

His mother came into the kitchen in time to hear the last part of that sentence. "Who will take our house?"

"The Bosniaks. They took his ball."

"The boys he plays with?"

"They won't let us play with them anymore."

"You didn't tell me that," his father said. "Since when?"

"A few weeks ago. They decided not to let Vasilije and me play with them."

"I don't believe it," his mother said. "How could the boys you've played with all your life suddenly decide not to let you play with them?"

"They're probably following the lead of their parents," his father said.

His mother shook her head sadly. "They also took your ball?"

"They didn't take it. A soldier did."

"A Bosniak soldier?"

"He doesn't know," his father said. "But it probably was. So I was saying it wouldn't be long before they took our house."

"I don't believe they will."

"They control this city. They can do anything they want."

"But why would they hurt us? We never hurt them."

"They have a grievance against Serbs."

"They never acted like they did."

"Well, things have changed."

"I don't believe," his mother said, "that people who are good can turn bad overnight."

"Maybe they weren't good," his father said. "Maybe they were bad all along."

"I don't believe that."

"Then how do you explain what's happening?"

"I think people are being misled."

"You mean by politicians?"

"Yes. They're stirring people up for their own purposes."

"Maybe they are. But they already started a war, and I don't see how we can stop it."

"We can stop their war by not getting drawn into it."

"So we should let them take Milos's ball?"

His mother nodded. "We shouldn't fight them over a ball. We can always buy another one."

"And what if they take our house?"

"They won't. We've lived here all our lives, and we've always gotten along with them."

"I think we should leave," his father said, "while we still have a chance."

"I don't want to leave. This city is our home."

Milos finally opened the book for his religion course. The assignment was on the origins of monotheism, and he was reading about the Pharaoh Akhenaten, who worshipped the sun god Aten as the only god, when his mind wandered.

He closed his eyes and saw Amira as he had seen her the first time, sitting with her lips still parted after responding to Sister Maura. He saw her leaving the classroom and walking down the hallway. He saw her emerging from her sociology class and gazing at him with those dark eyes. He saw her walking with him to the bus stop. In his imagination he wrapped his arms around her and held her close, saying: "I love you. I love you. I love you."

The past no longer mattered. Only the present and the future mattered.

Chapter 3

AMIRA, HER FATHER, and her brother Kashir were sitting at the table, having just finished eating the food they had brought home, when Uncle Ahmed came into the apartment. She immediately got up to get the money out of her backpack.

Uncle Ahmed sat down in the empty chair and asked Kashir how school was. Kashir, a sophomore at Yonkers High School, replied that things were going well.

"*Mrzim ti reći ovo,*" her father said to Uncle Ahmed. "Before we locked up the store tonight, something happened."

"What?" Uncle Ahmed said, looking concerned.

"Someone sprayed 'Muslims, go home' on the front window."

"Oh, no," Uncle Ahmed said sadly. "Nothing like that ever happened before."

"People blame us for the attack. They know we're Muslims, so they believe we're terrorists."

"People in the neighborhood have been coming to my store for years. They know we're not terrorists."

"But there are people who believe we are."

"When I was walking along South Broadway," Amira told her uncle, holding the money to give to him, "a man called me a dirty Muslim and said I deserved to die. So I don't wear my headscarf on the street."

"You didn't tell me that," her father said.

"I didn't want to upset you."

"It'll blow over," Uncle Ahmed said. "Americans are good people. A lot of them came here to get away from the same kind of thing."

"I wonder," her father said. "The way Bush is talking, it sounds like America is going to war against Muslims."

"It's not against Muslims, it's against terrorists."

"They equate Muslims with terrorists."

"No, they don't. And Bush apologized for using the word crusade. He didn't mean it."

"If he didn't mean it, then why did he say it?"

"I don't know. It was a slip of the tongue."

"When the tongue slips," her father said glumly, "the truth comes out."

"Here," Amira said, handing Uncle Ahmed the money.

After making a quick count he said: "We had a good day."

"We did," her father said, "until someone sprayed that message on the window."

"I assume you scraped it off."

"I did. But it might happen again."

"I don't think it will. But if it does, we'll report it to the police."

"And what will they do?"

"They'll watch the store. They don't want that kind of thing happening in the neighborhood."

Her father sighed. "I feel like we're still in Bosnia."

"We're not in Bosnia, we're in America."

Her father looked doubtful.

"What happened there," Uncle Ahmed said, "won't happen here. We may have people who hate each other, but we have laws that stop them from doing what they did there. And most people are decent here."

"That's what we thought about most people there."

"It's a whole different situation. We don't have ethnic groups here fighting over territory. And we don't have grievances that go back a thousand years."

"You're assuming that people who came here left their grievances behind."

"Well, I can't speak for other people, but I left my grievances behind. I don't think about the past, I think about the future. And so should you."

"Okay. I'll try," her father said.

Uncle Ahmed pocketed the money, and then he got up from the table, saying: *"Laku noć.* I'll see you tomorrow."

"Laku noć," Amira and her father said.

When Uncle Ahmed had left, Amira said: "You can't judge America by the action of one person."

"Two people. You have to count the man who called you a dirty Muslim."

"All right. But other people haven't acted badly toward us."

"What other people are you talking about?"

"The customers at the store."

"They need things from us, so they're not going to act badly toward us. But what about the kids at the college?"

"They don't know I'm a Muslim."

"They can't tell from your headscarf?"

"I don't wear it at the college."

"You don't? Your Aunt Malika won't like that."

"Unless you tell her, she won't ever know."

"I won't tell her. If you don't want to wear a headscarf, that's okay. I just don't want the wrong kind of boy to see what a beautiful girl you are."

"Don't worry," she said, beginning to worry.

"What about the kids at the high school?" her father asked Kashir, who had listened to them in silence.

"They don't even know what a Muslim is. And anyway they don't care what religion you are."

"Well, then maybe your uncle's right about America."

"He *is* right," Amira said. "It's not Bosnia."

After clearing the table she washed the dishes and put them away. Her brother had gone to his room, and her father was watching television. He had the news on, which helped him learn English. She stopped and stood next to his chair for a while, watching the scenes of devastation from the World Trade Center.

"I was wondering," her father said, "how they know who did it. I mean, their bodies must have been obliterated."

"They must have some evidence."

"What if they don't? What if they're only saying that Muslims did it?"

"Why would they lie about it?"

"To justify a war against us."

"Why would they want a war against us?"

"To protect Israel. In fact, I was wondering if the Israelis did it to frame us."

"Papa," she said, laying a hand on his shoulder. "I wish you would stop thinking about it. Whoever did it, they did an evil thing. And God will punish them."

"When I think about what they did to your mother, I tell myself that God will punish them. But it doesn't help."

"I know it doesn't. What helps is praying in the name of God, the Lord of Mercy."

He patted her hand. "You're a good girl. Your mother in heaven is proud of you."

"I hope she is. I love you, Papa." She kissed his head, and she left him, saying: "I have to go and study."

In her room she sat down at her desk and opened the book for her religion course. But she had trouble concentrating because the conversation with her father had stirred up memories.

Her last happy memory of Srebrenica was the party her father gave at his restaurant for her ninth birthday. Her family and many of their neighbors were there, including her best friend Farida, who lived a few houses down the street. She made sure that Farida and she got corner pieces of her cake, which had the most frosting.

A few days later the war started. At the time she had a general idea of what was happening, and it was only after they had come to America that she learned the details from her father. Without warning the Serbs began to attack the villages around Srebrenica, clearing them of Bosniaks in order to make them part of Serbia. Many survivors from these villages sought refuge in Srebrenica, but then the Serbs captured Srebrenica. Her family was planning to leave the city, but then Bosniak forces recaptured it, and they decided to stay there after the UN declared Srebrenica a safe haven and promised to protect it. They believed that with UN protection they would be safe, so they were surprised when the Serbs lay siege to the town. By then they were trapped. If they stayed they would starve because the town was cut off from food, but if they tried to leave they would be killed by snipers. And meanwhile they were bombarded by mortars.

One night there was a terrific crash that sounded like it was right on top of them. Their house shook, and some things fell over, but the shell hadn't hit them, it had hit a house down the street, and when they all went to see what had happened they saw the remains of what had been the house of their neighbors. Then a girl crawled out of the rubble impaled in her belly by a shaft of wood, screaming and writhing in unspeakable pain. It was Farida.

Amira's mother tried to shield her from the horrible sight by turning her away and covering her ears, but she still heard the cries of pain.

"In the name of God, the Lord of Mercy," her mother prayed when the cries had stopped.

The months passed, and by early summer people were dying of starvation. Then the Serbs began their offensive, the UN troops abandoned the city, the Bosniak forces retreated, and the Serbs recaptured Srebrenica.

Her family was fleeing by night to Potoćari when they met a young man who had just been there. He was bleeding from the side of his neck.

"What happened to you?" her father asked.

"They shot me," the young man said.

"The Serbs?"

"Yes. They're killing all Bosniak males of fighting age."

"How did you escape from them?"

"I pretended to be dead."

"What are they doing to the females?"

"They're putting them on buses to Kladanj."

"They're not mistreating them?"

"In some cases I think they are, but in most cases I think they're only sending them away."

"What about your family?"

"They killed my father, but they put my mother and my sisters on a bus."

"How old are you?"

"Nineteen."

"He's ten," her father said, indicating Kashir. "Do you think they'd harm him?"

"I wouldn't take him to Potoćari."

"Where would you take him?"

"I'd take him across the countryside, where I'm going. If we stay off the road, we might be able to slip by them."

"What do you think?" her father asked her mother.

"I think we should all stick together," her mother said.

"With due respect," the young man said, "I don't think women should go with us. I think you'll have a better chance on a bus."

"I think he's right," her father said. "If the Serbs catch us, they'll kill us. And if you're with us, they'll kill you too."

Frowning, her mother asked the young man: "Are any men allowed on the buses?"

"Only men who aren't fighting age, which rules out your husband and probably your son."

"So if we went with you," her father said, "we could get you into trouble."

"Well, I don't like the idea of splitting up the family," her mother said. "And what if we survive and you don't?"

"God will protect you," her father said. "But we'll have a better chance of surviving if we split up."

So they split up, and when Amira arrived at Kladanj without her mother she was put into a refugee camp, where she stayed for almost two months without knowing if her father and brother had made it through. When they finally arrived at the camp she had to tell her father what had happened to her mother.

"Oh, no," he cried, crumbling to his knees.

She put her arms around him and Kashir, trying to comfort them.

Five months later they arrived in America, where Uncle Ahmed and Aunt Malika welcomed them. Aunt Malika, her mother's sister, had two children of her own, but they were both boys, and she had always wanted a daughter, so she gladly took Amira under her wing.

Amira loved her aunt, and she appreciated the guidance she received from her. At times she felt that Aunt Malika was overprotective, and she wished she was allowed to do things that normal American girls did. But she could understand why Aunt Malika would be protective after losing her only sister and being responsible for the only girl in the family. What she couldn't understand was why her cousin Hasan was so protective.

Hasan was seventeen when she arrived, and from the moment when she met him the way he looked at her made her uneasy. If she hadn't known that cousins weren't supposed to have such feelings toward each other, she would have thought it was lust in his eyes. Instead, she attributed that look to an intense feeling of possession. She was *his* cousin, and if anyone tried to mess with her, he would protect her.

She would never forget the time when she was playing with two boys her age in the backyard a few months after she arrived, before she could speak much English. They were playing with a soccer ball, kicking it around, and then one of the boys picked it up and ran with it. The other boy chased him and pulled him to the ground.

They were both laughing and having such a good time that when one of the boys threw the ball to her, she ran with it, hoping they would pull her to the ground. When they did she rolled around with them, laughing.

At that moment Hasan came out of the house and yelled: "Stop it!"

She assumed he was yelling at her, but it turned out he was yelling at the boys.

"We're only playing," one of them said.

"I don't like you playing that way with my cousin."

"She's your cousin? She doesn't look like you."

"Luckily for her," the other boy said.

"What did you say?"

"Your cousin's lucky she doesn't look like you. If she did, she wouldn't be pretty."

Hasan lunged at the boy and smacked him.

"Hey, that hurt," the boy said, holding his hand to his face.

"Why did you do that?" the other boy asked.

"I don't like you talking that way about my cousin."

"Hasan," she said in Bosnian. "These boys are my friends."

"They're not your friends," Hasan told her. "They want to do bad things with you."

"Oh, don't be silly. They only want to play."

"I think we should go," the smacked boy said.

"Yeah. I agree," the other boy said.

"I'm sorry," Amira told them.

"It's all right. We'll see you at school."

She went into the house and into her family's apartment, avoiding Hasan. A half hour later Aunt Malika came down to their apartment, bringing a headscarf.

"I think it's time for you to start wearing this," her aunt said.

"What did Hasan tell you?"

"It doesn't matter what he told me. I think it's time."

"You don't want boys to notice me?"

"I don't want them to see how pretty you are."

"Why don't you?" she asked, not understanding.

"They'll want to do bad things with you."

"Then why don't American girls wear headscarves?"

"Their parents don't care what they do."

"But if I wear a headscarf, then people will think I'm not normal."

"They'll only think you're a good girl. And you *are* a good girl. Your mother in heaven will be proud of you—"

Amira knew what was coming next.

"—if you wear a headscarf."

She tried again to study, but she couldn't focus on the origins of monotheism, and she started thinking about Milos. She hoped she would see him before the next meeting of their religion class on Wednesday. That was such a long time to wait.

Restless, she got up and went through the living room, where her father was still watching television, and into the kitchen. She ran some water into the teapot, which she put on the stove. She found the tea in the cabinet and dropped a bag into her mug, which had "Amira" painted on it. Her aunt had found it in a shop in Queens, which had a lot more Muslims than Yonkers. They even had a beautiful mosque.

She was pouring hot water into the mug when she heard Hasan in the living room, talking to her father. She knew they wouldn't talk openly in front her, so she stayed in the kitchen and listened to them.

"Did you see who did it?" Hasan asked.

"No. I was in the kitchen cleaning up."

"Where was Amira?"

"She was in the store, but she didn't see who did it."

"She must have seen something."

"You can ask her."

"Well, I think we need to protect the store."

"Your father talked about reporting it to the police. I mean if they do it again."

"The police won't do anything. They blame us for the police and firemen who were killed at the World Trade Center."

"I hadn't thought of that," her father said.

"You have to understand these people. They never liked us, but now they hate us."

"So how would you protect the store?"

"Oh, I'd get some guys I know from the Bronx."

"What would they do?"

"They'd watch the store."

"Would you have to pay them?"

"Yeah," Hasan said, "but I wouldn't have to pay them much."

"What does your father think about the idea?"

"He doesn't like it. He thinks the feeling against Muslims will blow over. But it won't blow over, and it'll get worse when America goes to war against Muslims."

"You think that's going to happen?"

"I know it will. You only have to listen to Bush. He's spoiling for a war against Muslims."

"So if there's a war against Muslims," her father said, "you think it'll get worse for us?"

"Of course it will. Do you know how they treated Germans

during World War I? Or how they treated Japanese during World War II?"

"How did they treat them?"

"They trashed the German shops, and they put the Japanese into camps."

There was a long pause. "So if these guys were watching the store and they caught someone spraying a message on the window, what would they do?"

"They'd make him regret fucking with us."

"What exactly would they do?"

"They'd break his arm."

"If they did, then he'd want to get even with us."

"Maybe he would," Hasan said. "But I don't care what gang he belongs to, it wouldn't be a match for my gang."

At that point Amira had heard enough. She took the bag out of her tea and disposed of it in the garbage, and then she left the kitchen with her mug.

"There you are," Hasan said, giving her the look that made her uneasy. Hasan had grown into a big guy, and with his shaved head he looked tough. He had gone for a year to Westchester Community College, but he had decided that college wasn't for him, so he had gotten a job driving a food truck for a company in the Bronx. It paid well, and he talked about getting his own apartment. She hoped he would, so he wouldn't be around so much.

"I overheard what you said about protecting the store. And I don't like the idea."

"We should let people trash our store?"

"They didn't trash the store. They only sprayed a message on the window."

"Well, I don't like the message. And if we don't stop them, they'll do something worse."

"If you do anything to them, they *will* do something worse."

"So we shouldn't fight back?"

"No. We shouldn't."

"You're talking like a Christian. I guess that's from going to a Catholic college."

"I'm talking like a Muslim," Amira said staunchly. "In case you don't know, our religion is against war unless it's self-defense."

"Protecting our store is self-defense."

"So if your guys from the Bronx catch a guy spraying a message on the window of our store, what will they do him?"

"What do you think? They'll break his arm."

"They don't have to hurt him. They only have to stop him."

"What if he resists?"

"They should call the police."

Hasan laughed. "You don't understand anything."

"I understand more than you do. While you were safely living in America, I was in Bosnia seeing what happened there."

"Then you should want to fight back."

"I don't. I want to live in peace."

"Well, they won't let you."

"They will if I give them a chance."

"If you give them a chance," Hasan said with a leer, "they'll take advantage of you."

"No, they won't," she said, not liking his implication.

"Your father says you didn't see who sprayed the window."

"I only saw a motion across it."

"You didn't go out to see who it was?"

"I went out right after I put some food away, but by then he was gone."

Hasan made a face as if she was useless. "All right. I'll talk with my father about protecting the store."

When he had left, her father said: "I don't like the idea either."

"I know. I heard you."

"And he admits that his father doesn't like it. So it probably won't happen."

"I hope it doesn't. I don't want to be in another war."

"I don't either."

She took her mug of tea into her room and sat down at her desk to study. She read only a few paragraphs before she was distracted again by the voices of Hasan and Uncle Ahmed upstairs. She assumed they were arguing about Hasan's idea of protecting the store. She knew that as the head of the family Uncle Ahmed would make the decision. But she didn't rule out the possibility that Hasan would do it anyway. If no one sprayed a message on the window again, then Uncle Ahmed would never know the store was being protected.

Then she thought about how Hasan looked at her. From the way it made her feel she was sure that Hasan lusted for her. And that helped her understand why he had stopped the two boys from playing with her. Hasan had been jealous. And he would be jealous of any guy with whom she had a relationship.

Of course she didn't have a relationship with Milos—they had just met, and they hardly knew each other. But if she developed a relationship with him she would have to be careful not to let Hasan find out about it.

"Silly girl," she told herself again. She had to laugh at herself for thinking so far ahead of things. She had met a boy in class, she had walked with him to the bus stop, and she had talked with him a little, but here she was worrying about what her cousin Hasan would do if he found out about a relationship that didn't exist.

When she finally finished reading the assignment it was time to go to bed. She went to the bathroom and brushed her teeth, and then she said goodnight to her father, who was still watching television.

"Don't worry," she told her father. "God will protect us."

"I hope so," he murmured.

Before going to bed she said her evening prayer. She was supposed to say formal prayers five times a day, but she couldn't remember the last time she had done this. Their lives had been disrupted in Srebrenica, and when they came to America they were cut off from their community. There wasn't a mosque in Yonkers, and though there was a mosque in Astoria attended by Bosniaks, it took a while to get there in the Friday traffic so her family went there only on special occasions.

But she did say prayers three times a day: when she got up in the morning, around noon, and before she went to bed. She didn't follow the whole ritual, but she always recited the opening *surah* of the Quran: "In the name of God, the Lord of Mercy, the Giver of Mercy. Praise belongs to God, Lord of the worlds, the Lord of Mercy, the Giver of Mercy, Master of the Day of Judgment. It is you we worship; it is you we ask for help. Guide us to the straight path: the path of those you have blessed, those who incur no anger and who have not gone astray."

She always added a personal prayer, usually for her family, but tonight she asked God for peace in the world and a better understanding between Christians and Muslims. And she asked God to stop America from going to war.

As she lay in bed she thought about Milos. She imagined the two of them walking along the edge of the campus on the path that overlooked the river. They were holding hands, and the morning sun was lighting up the Palisades, the cliff on the other side of the river. It rose there like a wall that God had built to protect them from hatred.

Chapter 4

AS SISTER MAURA took attendance at the next meeting of her religion class she noticed that Milos and Amira were sitting next to each other. That was significant because students usually sat in the same seats they had taken in the first class, but Milos had moved next to Amira, displacing the student who had sat there before.

If students changed seats it didn't bother Sister Maura, as it would have bothered some of her colleagues who identified students by where they sat. A student had once confided to her that his class deliberately changed seats to confuse their professor.

Milos and Amira weren't looking at each other, but from the aura that emanated from them Sister Maura could tell that they were intensely aware of each other.

"All right," she said after she had finished taking attendance. "Maria, what is monotheism?"

"It's the belief in one god," Maria said.

"Only one god and no others?"

Maria paused. "Yes. Only one god."

"Sean, how was that different from previous religions?"

"In previous religions," Sean said, "they believed in more than one god."

"Can you give us an example?"

Sean looked blank.

"Can anyone give us an example?"

Tanya raised her hand.

"Yes, Tanya."

"The Greeks believed in a lot of gods."

"Good. Can you name a Greek god?"

"Aphrodite, the goddess of love."

"Very good. Can anyone else name a Greek god?"

Monica raised her hand.

"Yes, Monica."

"Athena, the goddess of wisdom."

"Excellent. We could go on, but the thing to understand is that in polytheistic religions there was a god for every human quality as well as for every natural phenomenon."

"Did the Greeks have a god of sex?" Joe asked.

"They did," Sister Maura said, not surprised by the question. She knew that of the things on their minds, sex was usually at the top. "His name was Eros."

"Is that where we get the word erotic?"

"That's right. Eros was the son of Aphrodite."

"What about the other kind of love?" Jessica asked.

"There's another kind of love?" Steve joked.

"What kind do you mean?" Sister Maura asked, ignoring Steve.

"The kind you have for your mother or father."

"Or for your neighbors," Tanya said.

"Or for God," Milos said.

"Good questions," Sister Maura said. "The Greeks had a word for that kind of love, but they didn't have a god for it."

"Why didn't they?" Jessica asked.

"I don't know. Maybe they didn't expect that kind of love from their gods."

"You mean their gods were like humans?"

"Yes. They had human weaknesses."

"Did the Greeks have a god of hate?" Amira asked.

"They did. Her name was Erida. She was the sister of Ares, the god of war."

"That makes sense," Jessica said. "Hate and war go together."

"Why did they make hate a woman?" Tanya asked.

"That's a good question," Sister Maura said. "Maybe because their religion was invented by men."

"Is that why," Tanya asked, extending her question, "when people decided there was only one god, they made him a man?"

"You believe God is a man?"

"Yeah. We pray to him like he's a man."

"I don't," Jessica said. "I pray to her like she's a woman."

"In a monotheistic religion," Sister Maura told them, "the one god no longer has the limits of gender, nor any other limits of being human. So the one god becomes the god of the kind of love you were talking about."

"What do we call that kind of love?" Amira asked.

"The Greeks called it *agape*. The Romans called it *caritas*. In English we have to say what kind of love we're talking about. The love a mother has for her children. The love a husband has for his wife. The love we have for our neighbors. The love we have for God."

"There isn't a word for each kind of love?"

"There isn't in English."

"I was just thinking," Milos said. "There are many different kinds of love, but there's only one kind of hate."

"That might explain the power of hate," Sister Maura said.

"But love can overcome hate."

"It can as long as it doesn't waver."

At that point Milos and Amira looked at each other as if they were making a solemn vow, and Sister Maura felt privileged to witness it.

Milos let her leave the classroom a few steps ahead of him and then he walked along with her, saying: "I was hoping we could meet sometime today."

"I have to be at work by two, and after work I have to go home with my father. So I don't know about today."

"What about tonight?"

Amira shook her head, saying: "I'm not allowed to go out at night. My family's very traditional."

"Well, what's your schedule on other days?"

"I have classes from ten until two-thirty-five on Tuesdays and Thursdays, so they're worse than Mondays and Wednesdays."

"What about Fridays?"

"I don't have classes, but I have be at home for prayers in the morning, and I have to be at work in the afternoon."

"Do you work on Saturdays?"

"Yeah. But only in the morning," she added encouragingly.

"Are you free this Saturday afternoon?"

"Yeah," she said after a moment.

"Could I go to your house?"

She shook her head. "I think it would be better if we met somewhere else."

"How about the library?" he suggested, wondering what the problem was.

"That would be fine. I go there on Saturdays."

They turned and headed down the long hallway, caught up in the stream of students.

"I wish," Milos said, "we could meet before Saturday."

"We can meet after class today."

"It's not enough time."

"Well, I don't know when else we can meet before Saturday."

He had an idea. "We could cut our next class."

"Oh, I don't know if I can do that."

"You don't have a test, do you?"

"No. But I haven't ever cut a class before."

"I haven't either. And we'd only do it this one time."

She was silent for a while, and then she asked: "Where could we go?"

"We could go on the path that overlooks the river."

"That's my favorite place on campus."

"It's mine too. What do you say?"

"All right," she said. "But just this one time."

"We won't do it again," he promised.

They turned around and headed in the other direction, not wanting to run into their professors. They went downstairs and out through a door that led to the athletic fields. At the far side of the baseball diamond was the path that overlooked the river. At the edge of the bluff was a wall built with the same type of gray stone that was used for the mansion of the estate, which a family named Morrissey had bequeathed to the college.

After leaving the athletic fields the path went through a grove of trees and crossed a stone bridge over a ravine carved by a stream that fed into the Hudson. On the other side of the bridge was a secluded spot that was used by residential students for nighttime parties, as evidenced by the occasional beer can or plastic container that littered the well-tended lawn.

Milos and Amira sat down where they had an unobstructed view of the river. The sun was shining, and there was only the slightest breeze. In the distance to the south was the skyline of the city, shrouded in smoke from the burning remains of the Twin Towers. They faced the awful sight together, observing a moment of silence.

"God have mercy," Amira murmured.

"God forgive them," Milos said.

They turned from the sight and faced the river, which reflected the wall of the Palisades on the other side. There wasn't a ripple to disturb the image.

"It's so peaceful here," Amira said, closing her eyes and lifting her face.

"It's the way the whole world should be."

"I liked what you said in class about love overcoming hate."

"I believe it can. But I don't see it happening."

"I don't either. In fact, things are worse since the attack. You know what someone did last night to my uncle's store? He sprayed a message on the window that said: 'Muslims, go home.' We were so upset."

That she was a Muslim didn't surprise him, nor did it matter. He loved Amira whatever her religion was. What concerned him was the fact that the message on the window was the same as the message on Bojan's bumper sticker. Granted, it was probably a standard message, but the coincidence made him wonder. "Did you see who did it?"

"No. We didn't. We were busy closing."

"Did you report it to the police?"

"No. If it happens again, my uncle says he *will* report it. But my cousin wants to stop it from happening again."

"How would he do that?"

"By getting some guys from the Bronx to watch the store."

"If they caught someone spraying the window, what would they do to him?"

"They'd break his arm."

"Your cousin sounds like a bad guy."

"He's as full of hate as whoever sprayed that message on the window."

"God help us. I thought we got away from the hate."

She was silent for a moment, and then she asked: "Where are you from?"

"Bosnia."

"You are? I am too."

"Where did you live in Bosnia?"

"In Srebrenica. I'm a Bosniak," she added.

Milos had heard what the Serbs had done to the Bosniaks in Srebrenica, and it made his heart go out to her. "What happened to your family?"

"My mother was killed," she told him in a low voice. "My father and my brother got out all right."

"I'm sorry," he said as if he was responsible.

"Are you a Serb?"

"Yeah," he admitted.

"You're not responsible. How old were you then?"

"I was almost thirteen."

"Where did you live in Bosnia?"

"In Zenica."

"Did Serbs control that city?"

"No. Bosniaks did."

She gazed at him with those dark eyes and finally asked: "What did they do to your family?"

"They destroyed my father's shop, and then they killed my mother's brother. My father and my mother, my grandmother, and my two sisters got out all right."

"I'm sorry," she said as if she was responsible.

"You're not responsible."

"But we have to know what happened in Bosnia so we can understand how our families feel."

"I can understand how they feel, but I don't feel like they do. I don't hate Bosniaks."

"I don't hate Serbs."

"I wish I could make them stop hating each other."

"I do too. But I don't know how."

"Well, maybe," he said, hoping, "if they see how we love each other, they'll realize that it's possible for Serbs and Bosniaks to love each other."

"Maybe they will," she said as if she wanted to believe it. "But what if they don't want us to love each other?"

"Then they won't want us to see each other. But they can't stop us. We're of legal age."

"They can still make it hard for us. So at least for a while I think it would be better if they don't know about us."

"Okay. We won't tell them about us."

They gazed into each other's eyes, and their faces were drawn together as if by a force stronger than gravity. Their mouths met in an exploratory kiss, and liking what they had found, they continued it.

"I never kissed a boy before."

"I never kissed a girl like that."

They kissed some more.

They had to walk fast to make it to the bus stop in time. Her bus came less than a minute after they got there, and they had to say a hasty goodbye.

As he rode down Executive Boulevard he closed his eyes and remembered how they had kissed each other, discovering how their mouths could unite them. He didn't see how he could live three whole days without seeing her.

He spent the next four hours in a daze, running items under the sensor at the checkout counter and at times forgetting where he was.

"Hello? Are you there?" a woman called to him with good humor. "You need to press the button so I get a receipt."

"Oh, yeah. I'm sorry."

"Don't be sorry. Just press the button."

He was finally brought to his senses by a young woman with food stamps, which you had to process manually. There were always some customers with food stamps, and this woman had a baby girl perched in her cart who smiled at him dreamily.

When he got home he found Bojan in the driveway, rubbing the hood of his pickup with a cloth. Mindful of what Amira had said about the message that someone had sprayed on her uncle's store, he decided to broach the subject with his cousin.

"I noticed your bumper sticker," Milos said, stopping in the driveway.

"You like it?" Bojan asked without looking at him.

"No. I don't. I think it's inappropriate."

"Inappropriate? Is that a word you learned in college?"

"No. I learned it in high school."

"Well, I don't care what you think. That sticker says how I feel about Muslims. And in case it's not clear," Bojan said, "I hate Muslims."

"Why do you hate them?"

"They drove us out of the city where our family lived for generations."

"They didn't drive *you* out. You left with your father, who wanted to get out of there."

"He knew that if he stayed, they'd drive him out."

"But he came here, and he did better."

"No thanks to them," Bojan said, rubbing the hood. He had a tattoo of the American flag on his bicep. "And in case you've already forgotten about it, they killed three thousand people at the World Trade Center."

"A gang of crazy men did that."

"They were Muslims."

"Well, they could have been Christians. The guy who killed those people in Oklahoma City was a Christian."

"I don't care what he did. I care what those Muslims did."

"But there are Muslims who live in Yonkers, who came here to get away from the hate just like we did. I hope you don't hate them."

"I do. I don't like having them in Yonkers."

"Have you acted on your feeling?"

"What do mean?" Bojan asked, examining the hood.

"Have you done anything to Muslims?"

Bojan raised his head and looked at him defiantly. "What if I have? Why should you care?"

"I don't want to see a repetition of what happened in Bosnia."

"Don't worry. There won't be any repetition. We outnumber them in America. We're going to drive them out of here."

"You didn't answer my question," he said after a pause. "Have you done anything to Muslims?"

Bojan scowled. "It's none of your business."

"It *is* my business. If the police catch you, they'll arrest you, and that'll hurt our family."

"What would they arrest me for?"

"A hate crime."

"There's no such thing."

"There is. And you could go to jail for it."

"Don't worry. They aren't going to arrest me for a hate crime."

Milos watched his cousin resume working on the hood. Caressing its surface with a soft cloth, Bojan acted as if he loved his truck more than anything in the world. "I just don't see what you get out of hating people."

"Try it," Bojan said. "You'll see."

"When you love people, you want them to love you back. Is that how hate works? You want people to hate you back?"

"It's better than having them not give a shit about you."

"It is? How? What satisfaction do you get?"

"You control how they feel about you."

"But hate leads to violence."

"What's wrong with violence?"

"If you'd still been in Bosnia when people started acting on their feelings, you'd know what's wrong with it."

"Well, I wasn't there, so I don't know."

"Then ask my father. He'll tell you."

Bojan said nothing, with his eyes fixed on the hood of his truck.

"Whatever you do," Milos said in parting, "don't spray any messages on stores. You might get caught."

From the look that Bojan gave him out of the corner of his eye Milos concluded that he had done it. And he prayed that Bojan would take to heart what he had said.

Inside the apartment he went directly to his room, not wanting to hear a diatribe against Catholics from his grandmother. Unlike Bojan, she had personally experienced injury from the people she hated, but he still didn't want to hear it. What he wanted was a quiet space where he could think about Amira.

Lying on his bed with his eyes closed, he tried to recall the feeling of being with her, talking with her, and exchanging kisses with her, but he just couldn't put out of his mind the fact that someone had sprayed a message of hate on the window of her uncle's store, and that his own cousin had probably done it. He hoped that Bojan wouldn't do anything like that again, but he worried about what would happen if he did. Amira had said her cousin was getting some guys from the Bronx to watch the store, and what if they caught Bojan spraying the window? What if they hurt him?

Milos was wondering what more he could do to stop Bojan from harassing Muslims when his mother came into his room.

"I thought you were studying," she said, approaching him.

"No, I was just lying here and thinking."

"About what?"

"About how some people hate other people."

His mother sat down on the edge of the bed and looked at him with tender concern. "Were you thinking about what happened in Bosnia?"

"I was thinking about what's happening here."

"What's happening here?"

"People are doing things to Muslims."

"What kind of things?"

"Well, I heard they sprayed a message of hate on the window of a store owned by Muslims, here in Yonkers."

"Did you see that on the news?"

"No. Someone at the college told me about it."

"That's terrible. It's what we came here to get away from."

"It's in our family," he said, deciding to tell his mother more. "I keep hearing from Baka how she hates Catholics."

His mother sighed. "She has reasons for hating them."

"I know what they did to her, but aren't we supposed to forgive what people do to us?"

"Yes. But some things are hard to forgive."

"Well, let me ask you— Do you hate Catholics for what they did to her?"

"No. I don't hate them."

"Do you hate Muslims for what they did to your brother?"

"No. I don't."

"Have you forgiven them?"

His mother paused. "I don't know. I guess I have because I don't hate them. But I can't forget it."

"I understand. I don't hate the boys who wouldn't let me play football with them, and I don't hate the soldier who took my ball. But I can't forget it."

His mother studied him for a while, and then she asked: "What's happening with you?"

"What do you mean?"

"For the past few days you've been acting different. Is it a girl?"

Unable to hide it, he mumbled: "Yeah."

"Where did you meet her?"

"At the college. She's in my religion class."

"What's her name?"

"If I tell you, will you promise not to tell anyone?"

"I promise."

"Okay. Her name is Amira."

His mother's eyes opened wide as if she was seeing the whole picture. "Is she the one who told you about the message of hate that someone sprayed on the window of a store?"

"It's her uncle's store. She works there after school."

"What kind of relationship do you have with her?"

"We love each other."

"What do her parents think about it?"

"She only has a father. Her mother was killed."

"Where was her mother killed?"

"In Bosnia. Her family's from Srebrenica."

"Oh, God," his mother said, raising her eyes as if to question His judgment in putting this boy and girl together.

"We fell in love before we knew where we were from," Milos told her. "And even if we *had* known, it wouldn't have made any difference to us."

"It shouldn't make any difference to you. But it will to some people. And I don't think the girl's father will like her being in love with a Serb."

"She doesn't intend to tell her father anytime soon."

"Well, I don't think you should tell *your* father anytime soon. You know how he feels about Muslims."

"I'm not worried about him. I'm worried about Bojan. Have you seen his bumper sticker?"

"Yes. I've seen it. I told his mother she should make him remove it. She tried, but he told her it's his truck, so he can put whatever message he wants on it."

"Then Uncle Goran should make him remove it.."

"I'll ask him to talk with Bojan about it."

Milos hesitated but finally said: "I think Bojan sprayed that message on the store."

"Why do you think that?"

"Because it was the message on his bumper sticker."

"But that could be a coincidence."

"It could be," Milos said, "but when I advised him not to spray any messages on stores he gave me a look that seemed to confirm my suspicion."

His mother sighed. "If you're right, then his parents should know about it."

"They must understand that what Bojan is doing could start a war between our families. And we don't need another war."

"No, we don't," his mother agreed.

The next day he hoped to see Amira in the hallway between classes, but he didn't see her, and since her last class ended at two-thirty-five he couldn't meet her then without being seriously late for work. So he went through the whole day without seeing her.

When he got home after work he noticed the pickup in the driveway, and it still had the bumper sticker, so Bojan's parents evidently hadn't been able to make him remove it.

Before going into his room Milos stopped in the kitchen, where he found his grandmother preparing dinner. It smelled like her lamb stew, which he liked a lot, and that made him more tolerant of her. In fact, if he had to choose between Baka and Bojan, he would take Baka. At least she only talked about her hate.

"*Kakav je bio fakultet?*" she asked him.

"It was fine. I had a great class in English today."

"I should take classes in English. Where could I find them?"

"The community college has a branch in Yonkers. You might find them there."

"If we only had a church in Yonkers, it would have classes in English." It was one of Baka's complaints that there wasn't a Serbian Orthodox church in Yonkers. The nearest one was St. Sava in New York City, where they occasionally went. There was also one in Paterson, New Jersey, where they had gone once, but they had to drive over the Tappan Zee Bridge to get there. As a substitute for the real thing they could go to St. Mary's, a Russian Orthodox church on North Broadway, near Shonnard Place.

"I'll see if the community college has a branch near here," Milos said, not wanting to get into a discussion about the lack of a Serbian church in Yonkers. He knew his mother would have said: "You don't need a church to worship God."

He managed to study for a while, though his mind kept wandering to Amira. He wondered what she was doing now. Was she still at work? Was she home with her family?

He tried not to worry about Bojan.

The main topic of conversation at the dinner table was that Bush was going to address a joint session of Congress later that evening on the subject of the terrorist attack. The family had mixed feelings about Bush, though they preferred him to Clinton, who had ordered the attacks against the Serbs in Kosovo.

"What do you think he's going to say?" Milos asked his father.

"I think he's going to declare war on the terrorists."

"Does he know who they are?"

"He should know. He's the president."

"If he knows so much," Jovana asked, "then why didn't he stop the attack?"

"That's a good question. Maybe he wanted them to attack us."

"Why would he have wanted that?"

"Because it takes a lot to get Americans into a war. It took the attack on Pearl Harbor to get them into a war with the Nazis."

"Was America on the side of Serbia?" Tijana asked.

"It was," Baka said, giving America credit for at least one thing it had done right. "But America didn't stop the Croats from killing us. Russia stopped them."

"Well, Russia has its own problems now with terrorists," his father said.

"Are they Muslims?" Jovana asked.

"Yeah. At least the terrorists from Chechnya are Muslims."

"They're not Muslims," Milos insisted. "People who believe in God aren't terrorists."

"You're right," his mother said. "People who believe in God know that whatever our religion we're children of God, and that God doesn't want us to hurt His children."

"That's what my professor said."

"Which professor?" his father asked.

"The one who teaches my religion course." He was discreet enough not to say in front of his grandmother that the professor was a Catholic nun.

"So we shouldn't think of Muslims as terrorists," his mother said. "We should think of them as people like us, who believe in a merciful and forgiving God."

"How do you know what they believe in?" his father asked.

"When I was a girl, my best friend was a Muslim. And I learned from her that their God is the same as ours. They only call Him by another name."

"That may be true about Muslims," his grandmother said, "but it's not true about Catholics. Their God is different."

"We all believe in the same God," Milos said.

"We all do," his mother agreed.

His father and his grandmother didn't look convinced, but they didn't pursue it. Instead, they let the girls take over the conversation. The subject was the concert that a hot rock star was giving at Madison Square Garden, and they really wanted to go to it.

When it was time for the president's address to Congress they all gathered in the living room to watch it. As usual the girls sat on the floor.

"My fellow citizens," Bush said, "for the last nine days, the entire world has seen for itself the state of our union, and it is strong." There was applause. "Tonight, we are a country awakened to danger and called to defend freedom. Our grief has turned to anger, and anger to resolution. Whether we bring our enemies to justice, or bring justice to our enemies, justice will be done."

"Šta je rekao?" Baka asked.

"He said we'll get justice," Milos said. "But I think he meant revenge."

"Justice, revenge—what's the difference?" his father said.

Bush thanked the world for its support, and then he addressed the questions that people were asking, beginning with "Who attacked our country?"

"The evidence we have gathered," Bush said, "all points to a collection of loosely affiliated terrorist organizations known as al Qaeda. They are some of the murderers indicted for bombing American embassies in Tanzania and Kenya, and responsible for bombing the *USS Cole*. Al Qaeda is to terror what the mafia is to crime. But its goal is not making money; its goal is remaking the world—and imposing its radical beliefs on people everywhere."

"Šta je rekao?"

"He said we were attacked by an organization known as al Qaeda."

Bush continued. "The terrorists practice a fringe form of

Islamic extremism that has been rejected by Muslim scholars and the vast majority of Muslim clerics, a fringe movement that perverts the peaceful teachings of Islam. The terrorists' directive commands them to kill Christians and Jews, to kill all Americans, and make no distinctions among military and civilians, including women and children. This group and its leader—a person named Osama bin Laden—are linked to many other organizations in different countries."

"Their leader's name is Osama bin Laden," Milos said.

"That's a Muslim name," his father said.

"There are thousands of these terrorists in more than sixty countries," Bush said. "They are recruited from their own nations and neighborhoods and brought to camps in places like Afghanistan, where they are trained in the tactics of terror. They are sent back to their homes or sent to hide in countries around the world to plot evil and destruction."

"He's talking about Afghanistan," Milos said. "He says al Qaeda has camps there."

"The leadership of al Qaeda has great influence in Afghanistan and supports the Taliban regime in controlling most of that country. In Afghanistan, we see al Qaeda's vision for the world. Afghanistan's people have been brutalized; many are starving and many have fled. Women are not allowed to attend school."

"I think he's going to declare war on Afghanistan," Milos said.

"If they attacked us, then we should declare war on them," his father said.

"They didn't attack us. Al Qaeda did."

"The United States respects the people of Afghanistan. After all, we are currently its largest source of humanitarian aid; but we condemn the Taliban regime. It is not only repressing its own people, it is threatening people everywhere by sponsoring and sheltering and supplying terrorists. By aiding and abetting murder, the Taliban regime is committing murder."

Bush then made a list of demands on the Taliban and said they weren't open to negotiation. "The Taliban must act, and act immediately. They will hand over the terrorists, or they will share in their fate."

"There it is," Milos said. "He gave them an ultimatum. He said that if the Taliban doesn't hand over the terrorists, we will attack them."

"God help us," his mother said.

Later, as he was lying in bed, Milos heard Bojan drive off in his pickup. It was after eleven, and he wondered where his cousin was going at that hour.

Chapter 5

AMIRA LAY IN bed that night thinking about Milos. She had hoped she would run into him in the hallway between classes, but she hadn't seen him. She had known she wouldn't run into him on the way to the bus stop because he had already gone to work. But she would meet him on Saturday at the library, God willing.

She had watched Bush's speech on television with her father and Kashir. She had been relieved to hear Bush say: "I also want to speak tonight directly to Muslims throughout the world. We respect your faith. It's practiced freely by many millions of Americans and by millions more in countries that America counts as friends. Its teachings are good and peaceful, and those who commit evil in the name of Allah blaspheme the name of Allah. The terrorists are traitors to their own faith, trying, in effect, to hijack Islam itself. The enemy of America is not our many Muslim friends. It is not our many Arab friends. Our enemy is a radical network of terrorists and every government that supports them."

Amira had translated these words for her father, and she felt he believed them until they had a visit from Hasan after the speech was over. Ostensibly, Hasan came to return a wrench that he had borrowed from her father yesterday, but she felt his timing wasn't coincidental.

"What did you think of the president's speech?" Hasan asked her father.

"I liked what he said about Muslims," her father said.

"You did? You believed it?" Hasan shook his head as if her father was naïve. "He only said it to appease his buddies in Saudi Arabia. But when he said there would be a crusade, he really meant it. He can't wiggle his way out of that."

"He talked about a war against the terrorists, not against Muslims."

"He said the enemy was any government that supports the terrorists. And that, for a start, means Afghanistan."

"He gave them a chance to hand over Osama bin Laden."

"He knows they won't. He knows they can't."

"So what's his next step?"

"His next step is to invade Afghanistan."

"Well, if they capture Osama bin Laden, then that will be the end of it."

"They won't capture him. They don't want to. They want a war," Hasan said, "and they won't stop in Afghanistan."

"Where will they go from there?"

"They'll go where the oil is. That's what the whole thing is about. They don't want Muslims to have all that oil. They want it for themselves."

Her father shook his head as if he didn't know what to believe, and after Hasan left their apartment she spent the next half hour reassuring her father that America would never fight a war for the purpose of taking oil away from Muslims.

"In the name of God, the Lord of Mercy," she prayed before going to sleep, "please stop America from going to war."

The next day she had no classes, which enabled her in theory to attend communal prayer at a mosque. In fact, since Kashir had school on Friday, and since Amira and her father were needed at the deli, and since it would have taken them a few hours to get to the nearest mosque and back, they prayed together in their living room early in the morning, and then Kashir went to school and Amira and her father went to work. Amira as usual felt good after their prayers, which ended with the salutation: "Peace and God's Mercy be with you."

Her father went to the deli ahead of her because he needed to prepare hot food for the rest of the day. Her aunt and uncle did their prayers in the early morning and then went to the deli because they had to be open for their regular customers and they didn't have anyone they could trust to run the business for them. Her aunt often lamented the fact that they no longer kept the traditions of their community, but in America she had become pragmatic about certain things, which unfortunately for Amira didn't include the appearance and the conduct of girls. Amira sometimes wondered if Aunt Malika would be more pragmatic about these issues if she had a daughter. At least Amira had won the argument over jeans, which she justified on the grounds that they completely covered her legs, though she wasn't allowed to buy jeans that her aunt thought were too tight and she still had to wear a top that draped loosely over her rear.

She was in the backyard, killing time before she headed for the deli, when her cousin Rafid joined her. Rafid was so different from Hasan that you never would have guessed they were brothers. He was lean, attractive, friendly, and considerate. He was only two years older than Amira, so he didn't act like her protector. He was majoring in marketing at St. Catherine, and he had a job as a waiter at an Italian restaurant on McLean Avenue that Uncle Ahmed had helped him get because he knew the owner.

"Did you hear what happened?" Rafid asked her.

"No." She was afraid. "What happened?"

"You know the guys that Hasan got to watch the store? Well, last night they caught a guy spraying the window."

"What did they do to him?"

"They broke his arm."

"Oh," she moaned, imagining the pain.

"At least they didn't kill him."

"But they didn't have to hurt him. They could have just held him and called the police."

"Those guys don't deal with the police," Rafid told her. "They're members of a gang."

"What happened to the guy whose arm they broke?"

"The police found him and took him to St. Joseph's hospital."

"I hope he'll be all right."

"Yeah, I do too. The guys took his wallet," Rafid added, "so Hasan got his name and address from his driver's license."

"Did he tell you anything about the guy?"

"He only told me the guy's a Serb."

Her heart stopped. "How does he know that?"

"The guy has a Serbian name."

She told herself there were a lot of Serbs in the New York area, so there was very little chance that the guy was any relation to Milos. But a voice with more authority than her own told her she should worry. "Did he tell you the name?"

"No. He didn't. And I don't care what the guy's name is."

Amira wouldn't have cared if it had happened a week ago, but now she had a reason to care. "So how does your father feel about it?"

"He's not happy," Rafid said. "He doesn't want a war with Serbs. But Hasan wants one. He hates Serbs."

"Why does he hate them?"

"I don't know. He has no reason for hating Serbs. They never did anything to him."

"I don't understand it."

"I don't either."

They were silent for a while, sharing their inability to understand why Hasan hated Serbs or why anyone hated another group of people for no reason.

Then she asked: "Do you think the guy will get even with him?"

"I think he'll get even with *us*. I mean, now he has a reason for hating us."

"When he sprayed that message on our window he must have already hated us."

"Then he has a reason for hating us more."

Imagining where it could lead, and how it would affect her relationship with Milos, she made a resolution, saying: "We have to stop it."

"How can we stop it?"

"By making them realize that getting even won't give them any satisfaction."

"Well, I don't have a good relationship with Hasan. In fact, I don't like him. But he's my brother, and I don't want him to get killed in a stupid war. So if you're going to try to stop it, let me know how I can help you."

"I will. Thanks."

When she got to the deli there was a police officer questioning Uncle Ahmed. She recognized him as a customer who sometimes came there in the afternoon for a black coffee, which he insisted on paying for. He was always nice to her.

"You have no idea who might have done it?" the officer asked.

"No. I told you," Uncle Ahmed said. "I wasn't here when it happened."

"The guy claims he was walking by your store when two guys jumped him. They took his wallet, so maybe they just wanted to mug him. But I don't get why they broke his arm. It's not what muggers usually do."

"It's not? What do they usually do?"

"If the victim resists, they beat him up. If he doesn't, they take the money and run."

"Well, maybe he resisted."

"Maybe he did," the officer said. "But I have a feeling they caught the guy trying to rob your store."

"When I opened this morning," Uncle Ahmed said, "I didn't see any signs of attempted robbery."

"He might not have gotten far enough to leave any signs."

"So why do you think he was trying to rob us?"

"I don't know. I just have a feeling they were trying to stop him from doing something."

Uncle Ahmed didn't say anything.

The officer made a note on his pad, and then looking at Uncle Ahmed he said: "With all that's happening, I can understand why you might hire your own protection. But it's not a good idea. It's better to rely on us."

"I totally agree," Uncle Ahmed said, avoiding a denial that he had hired anyone.

"Would you like some coffee?" Amira asked the officer.

The officer smiled. "Yes. Thanks."

She got him a coffee, black as usual, and she took the money he offered her despite Uncle Ahmed's gesture not to make him pay for it. While the officer was drinking the coffee Amira went outside and looked around. She stepped out into the street, and then she saw it lying on the grate where rainwater flowed down into the storm sewer. She went and picked it up, and as she had expected, it was a spray paint can that had evidently rolled into the street and down to the grate after being dropped. She took it into the store and offered it to the officer, saying: "I found this can outside on the street."

"Hey, look at that," the officer said, taking it and inspecting it. "This might explain why they broke his arm."

"But they shouldn't have hurt him," Amira said. "They only should have stopped him."

"Well, that's what happens when you get involved with gangs. They hurt people."

As soon as the officer had left the store Uncle Ahmed let out his steam in Bosnian, saying: "I told Hasan not to bring those guys here. Now, look what's happened."

"He doesn't understand," Aunt Malika said. "If you respond to violence with violence, it only leads to more violence."

"So what are we going to do about it?"

"We have to talk with him again and make him understand how what he's doing will hurt his family. But it might be too late. He might have already started a war."

"It's not too late," Amira said. "If the guy doesn't retaliate, then Hasan won't have any reason for taking it further."

"He better not take it further," Uncle Ahmed muttered.

"Do we know who he is?" Aunt Malika asked.

"Rafid told me he's a Serb," Amira said.

"How would Rafid know?"

"Hasan told him."

"Well, if he *is* a Serb," Aunt Malika said, "we have to stop them from fighting each other."

"How can we stop them?" Uncle Ahmed said. "We couldn't stop them in Bosnia."

"We're not in Bosnia," Amira said, "we're in America."

"So tell me how we could stop them here."

"There are Serbs at the college. There's one in my religion class," Amira said carefully. "He might know this guy."

"Yeah, he might. They stick together like we do."

"And if he does know him, maybe I could talk with the guy."

"What would you tell him?"

"I'd tell him we're all children of God, and God doesn't want us to hurt each other."

"Your mother in heaven is proud of you," Aunt Malika said with a film of tears in her dark eyes. "It might work."

"It might," Uncle Ahmed said, though he looked doubtful. "How does Hasan know the guy is a Serb?"

"They took his wallet," Amira said. "His name and address were on his driver's license."

"But how does Hasan know a Serbian name from a Bosniak name? He was only twelve when we left Bosnia."

"He probably got it from the internet," Aunt Malika said. "He knows the history of what happened there."

"I wish that Hasan would learn other things," Uncle Ahmed said despondently.

"I'll ask him to tell me the name," Amira said. "And then I'll talk with the Serb in my class."

"So how well do you know this Serb?" Aunt Malika asked.

"I know him well enough. From what he's said in our class discussions, I know he doesn't hate Muslims."

"Well, that's a start. I wish I knew that about Bush."

At that moment a customer came into the store, so they suspended the conversation.

Later, they talked about how business had fallen off since the attack on the World Trade Center. They had to admit that it wasn't only Serbs who hated them. Other people evidently blamed them for the attack.

"That's another reason," Uncle Ahmed said, "why I didn't want Hasan to bring those guys here. It's not good for business. If the guy they hurt is from this neighborhood, people will think we belong to a gang."

"And they won't like that," Aunt Malika said.

Concern for the business, which supported both families, made Amira feel even more urgency to stop the violence.

When they got home from work that evening Hasan was in the driveway doing something with his motorcycle. It was a huge machine, and it had taken Hasan years to save enough money to buy it. He kept trying to persuade Amira to get on the bike behind him and go for a ride, and she kept declining because she was afraid of it. She stopped in the driveway while her father went into the house with the leftover food they had brought from the deli.

"Hi," she said, approaching him.

"Oh, hi," Hasan said, giving her the usual look.

"I heard you caught the guy who sprayed our window."

"How did you hear that?"

"Rafid told me."

"He shouldn't have told you."

"I also heard he's a Serb."

"Yeah. He's a fucking Serb."

She restrained her feelings, not wanting them to get in the way of her mission. Casually, she asked: "What's his name?"

"Why do you want to know?"

"In case he comes into the store, I want to know who he is. He might try to hurt me."

"If he does, I'll kill him," Hasan snarled.

"It would be better if I avoided him. I don't want you to go to prison for killing someone."

"Well, don't worry. He wouldn't dare to hurt you."

"If you tell me his name, I won't tell anyone."

"Why should I tell you?"

"I'm your cousin."

He looked at her as if he really enjoyed the power of having information she wanted, and she had no doubt that he wanted something in return. Of course he wasn't going to get it, but at least for a while he could fantasize about it. He finally said: "All right. I'll tell you. But you have to promise not to tell anyone."

"I promise," she said, knowing she would break this promise. She was learning about the compromises people had to make in pursuit of their objectives.

"His name is Bojan Stojanović."

Aware of his stony eyes watching for her reaction, she tried to suppress it. Since the guy had the same last name as Milos they could be related to each other. And while their being related might be good for her mission of stopping the war, it wasn't good for her relationship with Milos.

Without blinking, she said: "Thanks."

"You better not tell anyone."

"I won't." She left Hasan and went into the house with turmoil in her heart.

She couldn't study, and she couldn't pay attention to what her father and Kashir were talking about at the dinner table. She kept wondering if Bojan and Milos were related, and she recoiled from the possibility that they were brothers.

Before going to sleep she prayed that they were not related so it wouldn't affect her relationship with Milos.

On Saturday, after working in the morning, Amira walked to Getty Square, where she blended into the mix of people shopping for food and clothes and household wares. She passed a store that sold Jamaican patties and then a store with produce in boxes on the sidewalk, including mangos and tubers she didn't know the names of. She heard people speaking Spanish and different forms of English, which she recognized as African and Caribbean.

She headed down Main Street and came to the library. It had been moved there twenty years ago from its old location on South Broadway at Nepperhan as part of an urban renewal project. People compared the present building, which had once been a department store, unfavorably with the old building, but Amira didn't care about the building as long as it had books. She had spent a lot of time there reading, and that had helped her learn English, so she appreciated the library, and she was glad that they were constructing a new library near the waterfront, which they said would be better.

She went to the floor where they had biographies and histories. She was meeting Milos there at one, and she was a half hour early, which gave her time to browse through the books. She was leafing through a biography of Marie Curie when she noticed Milos coming down the aisle. She felt a leap of joy in her heart.

"Hi," he said, looking very glad to see her.

"Hi," she said, putting the book down.

"Do you want to hang out here or go somewhere else?"

"Whatever you want, it's fine with me."

"Well, the place where I usually hang out is occupied, so why don't we go for a walk?"

"Okay." As long as they could talk in private she didn't care where they went.

They left the library and headed down Main Street toward Warburton Avenue. Ahead of them she could see the waterfront with the Palisades across the river.

"Remember how I told you," she began, "that my cousin was getting some guys from the Bronx to watch the store?"

"Yeah," he said as if he had a sense of what was coming.

"Last night they caught someone spraying a message on the window."

"What did they do to him?"

"They broke his arm."

"Oh, God," he said with anguish.

"They took his wallet, so my cousin has his name and his address." She paused, having trouble saying it. "His last name is the same as yours."

"What? It's Stojanović?"

"Bojan Stojanović."

"Oh, God," he said with even more anguish.

"Is he a relative?"

"He's my cousin."

"How close are you to him?"

"We live in a two-family house that his father owns. I see him almost every day."

"What kind of relationship do you have with him?"

"I don't have a good one. I don't like him."

They stopped to wait for the light at Warburton. Some people joined them on the corner, so they stopped talking.

When they had crossed the street and regained their privacy she asked: "Do you think he'll want to get even with us for breaking his arm?"

"Of course he will. That's how he is."

"Then my cousin will get even with him."

"We have to stop them," he said with urgency.

"Yeah, we do. We don't want a war between our families."

"My parents and my cousin's parents don't want a war. They had enough war in Bosnia."

"My father and my cousin's parents don't want a war either. So it's only our cousins who want a war."

"It's only one of my cousins," he said. "My other cousin doesn't want a war."

"My other cousin doesn't want a war either."

At this point they were approaching the post office, whose main entrance was on Buena Vista, around the corner.

"So how can we stop them?" he wondered aloud.

"We can stop them," she said, "by making them realize that if they continue their war it will hurt their families."

"Yeah, we can tell them that, but will they believe it?"

They turned the corner and walked by the front of the post office toward Larkin Plaza, where a few stray men who looked homeless were sitting on the benches.

"Your cousin sprayed our window," she said, "and my cousin broke his arm. So maybe we can convince them that they're even now."

"My cousin has the next move," he said, "and if I can stop him that might be the end of it."

"Do you think it might help if we talked with him together?"

Milos considered the idea. "It might. It might get him to see that Muslims are human like he is. But then it might give him another reason for hating your family. I mean, he won't like it that I'm in love with a Muslim girl."

"I understand. Do you think it's worth the risk?"

"Yeah. I don't have any other ideas."

"Of course," she said after thinking about it, "if we decide to talk with him together, we have to tell our families about us."

"I already told my mother about us," Milos said. "She doesn't have a problem."

"I haven't told my aunt. She won't have a problem with your being a Serb, but she *will* have a problem with my having a boyfriend."

"Could she stop you from seeing me?"

"No. She couldn't. But she could give me a hard time."

"What about your father?"

"He'd be easier."

"So neither your aunt nor your father would have a problem with my being a Serb?"

"Well, they'd be happier if I fell in love with a Muslim boy, but once they got to know you they'd love you."

"My father and mother would love you too."

"So it's only our cousins who have a problem."

"It doesn't make sense," Milos said as they headed toward the fountain in the middle of the plaza. "Our parents have reasons for hating each other, but our cousins don't have any reasons. Yet our cousins are the ones who hate each other and want a war."

"They haven't been in a war," she said. "They don't know what it's like."

"But they've heard from their parents what it's like. Isn't that enough for them?"

"I guess it isn't. They can't imagine what it's like."

They stood by the fountain, watching the water rise and fall.

"So where does it come from?" Milos asked.

"You mean their hate?"

"Yeah, where does it come from?"

"I don't know. I only know where *my* hate came from. I hated Serbs for killing my mother. I hated them with all my heart."

"Do you still hate them?"

"No, I don't. Not anymore."

"What made you stop hating them?"

"Loving you," she said, putting an arm around his waist.

"And that's what made me stop hating Bosniaks for driving my family out of Zenica," he said, putting an arm around her waist. "Loving you."

"So we know how to stop hating people."

"Yeah, we do. But how do we get our cousins to stop hating each other?"

Gazing at the fountain, she felt the answer rise in her heart. "We get our cousins to understand that they're children of God, which makes them brothers."

"So that's our mission?"

"That's our mission." She couldn't put it into words, but she felt they should formalize their mission and as she watched the water falling from the fountain she had an idea. She broached it by saying: "In your religion they baptize you with water, right?"

"Right. They use water to wash away our sins."

"So let's use this water to wash away whatever might remain of our hate." She put out her hand and caught some water and brought it to his forehead. "Is that how they do it?"

"Yeah," he said. He gently did the same for her.

They exchanged kisses on the wet spots on their foreheads, pledging their love and their faith to the mission of peace.

Chapter 6

WHEN MILOS GOT home he found Bojan in the backyard sitting in one of the folding chairs the families used when they ate outside. His right arm was in a cast, supported by a sling, and his left hand held a can of Bud. A few crumpled cans lay on the patio near his feet.

"What happened?" Milos asked as if he didn't know.

"Oh, I was on McLean Avenue," Bojan told him, sounding aggrieved, "and I was attacked by a gang of Muslims."

"For no reason?"

"They had a reason. They hate Serbs."

"They knew you're a Serb?"

"They know who I am."

Milos sat down in a folding chair. "You didn't do anything to piss them off?"

"I didn't do anything. I was minding my own business."

"What were you doing on McLean Avenue?"

"I was getting a pizza."

"When was this?"

"Last night."

"Did they rob you?"

"Yeah. They took my wallet," Bojan said. "But that's not why they attacked me."

"Why did they attack you?"

"Because I'm a Serb. They're members of a gang in the Bronx."

"So what were they doing in Yonkers?"

"They were looking for Serbs."

"There aren't a lot of Serbs in Yonkers. If there were, we'd have a church here."

Bojan didn't comment. He finished the beer and crumpled the

can with his left hand as if he was demonstrating his strength. He dropped the can and reached for the six-pack at his feet. He popped open another can of beer and said: "They'll pay for what they did to me."

"You're going to take on a gang from the Bronx?"

"I know some guys who'll help me. They hate Muslims."

"Why do they hate Muslims?"

"For the same reason that we all hate them," Bojan said after gulping some beer. "The fuckers attacked us. They killed three thousand people at the World Trade Center."

"The guys who did that were terrorists."

"They were *Muslims*," Bojan said with rising anger. "And they were following their religion, which tells them to kill us."

Milos shook his head. "Their religion doesn't tell them to kill people."

"Yeah, it does. It tells them to go to war against people of other religions."

"It doesn't tell them to go to war. They have the same attitude toward war as Christians do. They're against war, except in self-defense."

"So they attacked the World Trade Center in self-defense?" Bojan said derisively.

"No, they didn't. But those guys weren't Muslims."

"Yeah, they were. And so were the guys who attacked me. They were Muslims. Now don't tell me that those fuckers attacked me in self-defense."

"They might have," Milos said. "They might have wanted to stop you from doing something."

"They wanted to stop me from getting a pizza?"

"They wanted to stop you from what you were going to do to that store."

With smoldering eyes Bojan asked: "What the *fuck* are you talking about?"

"I'm talking about spraying a message on their window."

"Where did you get that idea?"

"I got it from the people who own the store."

"What? You know them?"

"I know a member of the family."

"You hang out with Muslims?" Bojan said, squeezing the can to a point where the beer rose through the opening.

"We have students from all religions at the college."

"I thought it was a Catholic college."

"It is, but it welcomes everyone."

Bojan made a face of disgust. "I never thought my own cousin would hang out with Muslims. So what did they tell you?"

"They told me someone sprayed a message on their window."

"What did it say?"

"What your bumper sticker says."

"That doesn't prove I did it."

"No. It doesn't. But they caught you doing it again."

"And you believe them? Whose side are you on?"

"I'm not on *their* side when they break your arm," Milos said, "but I'm not on *your* side when you spray a message of hate on their window. I'm on the side of love and peace."

"Love and peace?" Bojan laughed at him scornfully. "We can't have peace with Muslims."

"Why not? We had peace with them before."

"We can never have peace with them. The only solution is to kill them all."

"Why do you hate them?" Milos asked, trying to understand. "What did they ever do to you?"

"They drove my parents out of Zenica."

"Your parents left before anything happened."

"If they hadn't left, the Muslims would have driven them out."

"Whatever made them leave Zenica, your parents don't hate Muslims."

"They claim they don't, but they really do."

Hoping to undermine this statement, Milos asked: "Do your parents know what you were doing when those guys caught you?"

Bojan tensely shook his head. "No. They don't know."

"If they knew, would they still be on your side?"

"You better not tell them," Bojan said, revealing a weakness.

"I won't tell them," Milos promised, forbearing to use the leverage he had just gained. And he didn't place a condition on his promise because that would have made it a threat. He wanted to lead Bojan to peace without using any kind of threat. "But I want you to stop hating Muslims. They're children of God, just like we are."

"They have a different God."

"They don't. They have the same God. They only have a different name for Him."

"What do you know about their religion?"

"I know a lot about it from my religion course." While they hadn't gotten to the part on Islam, he had read ahead in the textbook to learn about Amira's faith.

After a silence Bojan asked: "What do you expect me to do?"

"I expect you to do nothing. You sprayed their window, and they broke your arm. You're even now, so that should be the end of it."

"We're not even. Breaking my arm is much worse than spraying their window."

"There's no way you can make things exactly even."

Bojan glowered. "So you expect me to let those fuckers get away with breaking my arm?"

"If you get even with them," Milos said, "then they'll get even with you, and sooner or later your war will hurt our family."

"How do you know?"

"While you were safe in America, I was in Bosnia, so I know what it's like to be in a war. And I know what this war between you and my girlfriend's cousin might do to our family."

Bojan slowly drained the rest of his beer, and then he said: "I'll think about it. But I don't see how I can let them get away with it."

"Try," Milos urged him. "You'll see."

The next day was his mother's birthday, and since it was a special occasion the two families went to church at St. Sava, the Serbian Orthodox cathedral, which was in the city on West 25th Street between Broadway and Sixth Avenue. They drove there from Yonkers in two cars, with five people in each car, and Milos volunteered to ride with Uncle Goran so that his sisters could ride with his father, his mother, and his grandmother. He sat in the back with Bojan and his brother Pamet, and being the youngest, Milos had to accept being sandwiched between them. Luckily, Pamet wasn't broad like Bojan, so they weren't too crowded.

Pamet, who was two years older than Milos, was sensitive and artistic, with a talent for drawing that he hoped would lead to a career in fashion design. He was in a program at the Fashion Institute of Technology, taking the train to the city for classes four days a week. He was in the city most of the time, and he often spent the night there with friends, so Milos didn't see him as much as he used to. They had always been close, and for the past few years they had been bonded by the secret that Pamet had shared with Milos and with no one else in their families, which was that Pamet was gay. Of course Bojan was the last person that Pamet would want to know his secret, and sitting between them on the way to the city, Milos felt like a buffer in more than the physical sense. Not having any common interests, the two brothers didn't say much to each other during the trip, and they didn't even use Milos as a conduit. In fact, Bojan stared out the window while Pamet told Milos about a musical he had seen on Broadway in which the costumes had been fantastic.

Since it was Sunday morning they had no trouble finding parking places on the street, and they walked to the church with Uncle Goran and Milos's father leading the way, followed by his mother, his grandmother, and Aunt Vidra, then the girls, and finally the boys. The girls talked the whole time, while the boys were mostly silent.

The church was gothic, with brownstone walls and a rose window over the entrance. Inside, it had a high vaulted nave with stained glass windows. According to his mother, it was originally an Episcopal church and was purchased by the Serbian community in the 1940s.

The two families filled a pew about halfway toward the altar, and they waited in respectful silence for the Divine Liturgy to begin. For a while it looked as if there wouldn't be many people attending, but everyone arrived at the last minute and by the time the clergy appeared the pews were almost filled.

The priest began the Great Litany by saying: "Blessed is the kingdom of the Father, and of the Son, and of the Holy Spirit, now and ever, and unto the ages of ages."

"Amen," the people said.

"In peace let us pray to the Lord," the priest said.

"Lord, have mercy," the people said.

"For the peace of God and the salvation of our souls, let us pray to the Lord."

"Lord, have mercy."

As the prayers continued, Milos hoped they would have a positive effect on Bojan, who was standing on the other side of Pamet at the end of the pew.

"For all those who commit injustices against their neighbors, whether by causing sorrow to orphans or spilling innocent blood or by returning hatred for hatred, that God will grant them repentance, enlighten their minds and hearts and illumine their souls with the light of love even towards their enemies, let us pray to the Lord."

"Lord, have mercy," Milos said, feeling that this prayer was especially appropriate.

It was a long service, with the Great Litany followed by the First Antiphon, a Little Litany, the Second Antiphon, another Little Litany, the Third Antiphon, and so on. By the time they got to the Little Entry, the girls were getting restless and the other boys looked as if they had tuned out, but Milos followed every word through the readings of the Epistle and the Gospel, the Litany of the Faithful, the Great Entry, the Litany of Fervent Supplication, the Confession of Faith, and finally the Eucharist. At the end of the service the priest said: "The blessing of the Lord be upon us, through His grace and love for mankind, always, now and ever, and unto the ages of ages."

As they walked slowly out of the church Milos joined his

mother and put his arm around her shoulder, knowing she had liked coming there.

"I wish we could come here more often," she told him.

"Maybe we can. We just have to get everyone up."

"It's not easy, especially with the girls."

They were going to have lunch at a Greek restaurant owned by a Serb from Belgrade whom Uncle Goran had met when they were recent immigrants. The restaurant was on Sixth Avenue, a few blocks from the church, so the two families walked there, again led by Uncle Goran and Milos's father. When they arrived they were greeted by the owner, who had set up a table for ten and reserved it for them. Uncle Goran sat at the head of the table and the boys sat at the foot.

The meal began with platters of Greek and Serbian food including salad, stuffed grape leaves, and sausages known as *cevapi*, which vanished so fast that Uncle Goran had to order another platter. The parents drank wine and the children drank soda, except for Bojan, who was old enough to order a beer. The conversation had started with Baka wishing they had a Serbian church in Yonkers so that they could go there every Sunday, and the parents talked about church for a while, and then the conversation fragmented with the men, the women, the girls, and the boys talking about different subjects.

The boys talked mostly about sports, with the main focus on the Yankees, who had lost to Baltimore the day before and were playing them today. The only question was when the Yankees would clinch the division title. Since baseball wasn't part of the culture in which they were raised, and they hadn't ever played it, their interest in the sport, which they had acquired in the process of being Americanized, was superficial. The sport they really cared about was football, which in America they had learned to call soccer, and after a perfunctory discussion of the Yankees, their interest gravitated toward soccer, and they seriously analyzed the prospects of Brazil, Italy, Germany, and France in the World Cup, which was being held the following year in Korea and Japan. They agreed that the Serbian team no longer had much chance of qualifying after failing to defeat Slovenia a few weeks ago, but they thought the United States still had a chance, though it had recently lost to Costa Rica.

They kept talking through the main courses of lamb and fish, which included a lamb and spinach stew called *jagnjeća kapama*, though on the menu it had a Greek name. Milos had two helpings of that, and he sat back and waited for dessert, which probably would be *baklava* and *palačinke*. At that point Bojan went out to have a cigarette, leaving Milos and Pamet together.

"What's going on with him?" Pamet asked as if he was worried.

"Don't you know?" Milos said. "He's fighting a war against Muslims."

"What does he know about them? He never met one."

"Maybe that's the problem. If he met one, he'd know they're people like us."

"I have one in my design course. He's really cool."

"I have one in my religion course. She's really beautiful."

"You sound like you're in love."

"I am. But there's a problem."

"There is? What is it?"

Milos hesitated, remembering that he had promised not to tell Bojan's parents why he had been attacked by those guys from the Bronx, but he saw an opportunity to get Pamet to work on his brother. "I'll tell you if you promise not to tell your parents."

"I promise," Pamet said, looking intrigued.

"This girl's family owns a deli in Yonkers, and Bojan sprayed a message on their window. It said what his bumper sticker says."

"Oh, shit. What made him do that?"

"Hate," Milos said. "Bojan hates Muslims. And I don't know where he got it from. I never heard it from your parents."

"They don't hate Muslims. In fact, my dad says the best thing that ever happened to him was getting out of Bosnia and coming to America."

"So he didn't get it from your parents."

"Well, there's a lot of hate in America. Maybe he got it from people here."

"Maybe he did. But wherever he got it, we have to stop him from acting on it."

Pamet looked as if he understood. "He told me some guys attacked him. So they attacked him because they caught him spraying the window?"

"They didn't catch him the first time. They caught him when he went there to do it again."

"And now he wants to get even with them?"

"Yeah, he does. But he can't do that by himself, so he'll get some guys to help him."

"Oh, no. You'd think that getting his arm broken would teach him a lesson."

"It didn't. It only made him hate them more."

Pamet sighed. "This sounds like what happened in Bosnia."

"I talked with him yesterday. I tried to make him understand that if he gets even with them, sooner or later his war with them will hurt our family."

"Did he understand?"

"He only said he'd think about it. So will you talk with him?"

"Sure I will. I don't want him to drag our family into a war. I didn't experience it like you did, but I can imagine how horrible it was."

"I don't think he can imagine it."

"Yeah, that's his problem. My brother has no imagination."

"I guess if you can't imagine how other people feel, you don't have a problem hating them."

"If he found out I'm gay," Pamet said, "he'd hate me. Now, that's a way I could divert him from hating Muslims—by activating his hate for gays."

Milos laughed, as he was supposed to, but he was dismayed by the possibility that Bojan's hate for one group of people could be replaced only by his hate for another group. He still hoped it could be replaced by love.

He saw Amira in religion class the next day. By now they had started reading about Judaism, beginning with the story of Genesis.

Sister Maura opened the discussion by saying: "Judaism is the oldest major monotheistic religion. Since it's monotheistic, there's only one God, and He's concerned with the people He created. He gave them ten commandments, which constitute the covenant or agreement between God and His people."

Milos raised his hand.

"Yes, Milos."

"I know I'm getting ahead of things, but next we're going to study Christianity and then Islam, which are all monotheistic religions. So Jews, Christians, and Muslims all worship only one God. Correct?"

"Correct."

"Do we all worship the same God?"

"I'll answer you with a question," Sister Maura said. "If we all worship only one God, could we have different Gods?"

"Well—" Milos considered.

"Yeah, we could have different Gods," Steve said. "Those other religions could have the wrong God."

In a mild voice Sister Maura asked: "If there's only one God, then how could they have the wrong God?"

Milos understood. "So we all must have the same God."

"We may have different names for God, but we all have the same God."

"Then why do people fight over religion?" Eduardo asked.

"That's a good question. Why do you think?"

"They don't understand other religions?"

"That's one reason."

"They don't understand," Amira said, "that we're all children of the same God."

"They don't do what God commands," Milos added. "They don't love one another."

Sister Maura smiled. "That's right. If they did, we wouldn't have wars."

"Are we going to have a war with Afghanistan?" Maria asked.

"From what the president said last Thursday, it looks like we're going to have a war."

"Do you think it's right to have a war?"

"I'll give you some criteria to decide for yourselves," Sister Maura said. "First, were we attacked, and was the damage lasting, grave, and certain?"

"We were, and it was," Steve said.

"Second, have we tried every alternative to war?"

"We gave them a chance to hand over Osama bin Laden."

"Do you think the Afghan government is in a position to hand him over?"

"I don't know. They should be."

"I don't think they are," Tanya said.

"Third, if we invade Afghanistan, do we have a reasonable chance of success?"

"How would you define success?" Eduardo asked.

"How would *you* define it?"

"Capturing Osama bin Laden," Steve said.

"What do you think our chances are?"

"I think they're good."

"I don't think they're very good," Tanya said. "He's hiding in the mountains. We'll never find him."

"Fourth, would a war do things to them that are worse than what he did to us?"

"It depends on what we do to them," Steve said.

"If we invade Afghanistan," Tanya said, "we'll kill thousands of people, and most of them will be civilians."

"The people he killed in the Twin Towers were civilians."

"But if we kill ten or twenty times as many civilians as he did, we'll do things to them that are worse than what he did to us."

"So what do you think?" Sister Maura asked them.

"I think a war is justified," Steve said.

"I don't think it is," Tanya said.

"I think it would be morally wrong," Milos said.

"I do too," Amira said.

"How many think a war would be wrong?"

All but two of the students raised their hands.

"Well, let's see what the president does," Sister Maura said. "May God help him."

When the class was over Milos followed Amira out, and they headed down the hallway along with a lot of other students.

"I was thinking about Sister Maura," he said. "I was wondering if she could help us."

"How could she help us?" she asked.

"Well, she's not a Bosniak, and she's not a Serb, so she's not on either side."

"Yeah. Then she could be a neutral referee."

"That's what I was thinking." They continued down the hall toward the room where Amira had her next class. "When I got home after seeing you, I talked with Bojan."

"How did it go?"

"I made some points," Milos said, recalling the highlights of the conversation. "And I found out that he doesn't want his parents to know what he's doing."

"That's good to know."

"It is, though I promised not to tell them. I didn't want to threaten him."

"I understand."

"He wants to get even with your family for breaking his arm, but I tried to convince him that if he continues his war with your cousin, sooner or later it'll hurt our family."

"Did you convince him?"

"I don't know. At least he said he'd think about it."

They stopped at the door to her classroom and lingered outside it. He was drawn toward her by a magnetic force, but since there were people all around them he resisted the urge to kiss her, and when they parted he held out a palm and gently touched it to the palm she held out.

He was waiting there for her after his biology class, and they walked together out of the building and toward the bus stop. Unable to accept the fact that because of their class and work schedules as well as their family obligations, they could only see each other for two short intervals on Mondays and Wednesdays and for a few hours on Saturdays, he said: "I wish we could see each other more often."

"I do too. But I don't see how we could."

"I do. If you were allowed to go out at night—" He stopped there and went no further.

Amira considered the idea. "I'd have to get permission from my father and my aunt."

"Your father's permission wouldn't be enough?"

"My father wouldn't give me permission without getting hers."

"Then ask for their permission."

"Well, they'd want to know all about you. And they'd want to meet you."

"So why don't I just come to your house?"

"If you did," she said, "then Hasan might see you."

"I hope you don't need *his* permission."

"No, I don't, but Hasan was always jealous of the boys I had relationships with."

"I thought you never had a boyfriend before."

"I never did, but when I was only a little girl Hasan was jealous of the boys I played with."

"He needs to get over his problem."

"I know he does, but this isn't a good time to deal with it. I mean while he's at war with your cousin."

"I understand. But if they weren't in a war, would there be any reason why I couldn't just come to your house and meet your parents?"

"No. There wouldn't be."

"So we have to make our cousins end their war."

By now they had reached the bus stop, and they waited there. Another girl joined them, and then two guys joined them. Unlike most students, they weren't carrying backpacks for their books and notepads. In fact, they weren't carrying anything. And their heads were shaved, their arms were tattooed.

When the bus arrived the two guys waited politely for the two girls to get on first, and then they got on. At the last moment Milos had a sudden urge to jump on the bus, but the doors closed before he could move, and he watched it lumber down Broadway with a helpless feeling of trepidation. If those guys had been sent to follow Amira, their orders must have come from Bojan, and their purpose must have been to find out where she was going. If they tracked her to the deli, then Bojan would know who told Milos what had happened there, and Bojan would know that Milos had a personal reason for not wanting a war between the two families, which would undermine his moral authority.

After entering the A&P he stopped at the pay phone and called information to get the number of the deli. He knew its name because on Saturday he had asked Amira. Her uncle had bought the business from an Italian family, and wanting to keep their customers as well as to avoid the costs of changing the name on documents, he had kept the name, which was Joe's Deli. In the present situation it was lucky he hadn't changed the name to Ahmed's Deli.

He got the number of the deli and dialed. As the phone rang he hoped and prayed that Amira would answer. If her aunt answered he would have to make up a story about how he was a student in her sociology class who needed her notes for an upcoming test, and if her aunt asked for his name he would have to give her an Irish or Italian name. At the last second he decided to borrow the name of a classmate, Mike Conroy.

"Joe's Deli," said a voice he recognized as Amira's.

"Hi. It's Milos," he said, relieved. He was thankful not only that she had answered but also that she had gotten there safely, which made him realize that even though he hadn't believed those guys would harm her, still he had been worried about her.

"How can I help you?" she said, pretending he was a customer. Evidently, her aunt was somewhere nearby and able to hear the conversation.

"I'm just calling," he said, "to make sure you got there safely. I saw two guys get on the bus right after you, and it looked like they were following you."

"They were," she said in a low voice, and then: "On a wedge?"

"So they know where you work."

"Yes. With lettuce and mayo?"

"I think my cousin sent them to follow you."

"I understand. And tomato?"

"I don't believe those guys would harm you. I think my cousin only wanted to find out who told me what happened at your deli."

"Okay. You can pick it up in about ten minutes."

"I'll see you tomorrow at the college."

"Okay."

"I love you."

When she didn't say "I love you too" he knew for sure that her aunt was listening.

The long rays of the setting sun were reaching between the houses on Woodland Avenue as he walked home. He was in front of a neighbor's house when he spotted Bojan in the driveway talking with the two guys who had followed Amira.

They evidently hadn't spotted him, so he ducked behind the neighbor's house and waited for them to go away. It took them long enough for a late-summer fly to discover him and bother him, but repeatedly shooing the fly away, he kept his position and stayed out of sight.

Finally, the two guys swaggered to the street and got into a black car and drove away with a blast that sounded like a leaf blower.

Milos came out from behind the house and strolled into the driveway as if he was just arriving from work. He greeted his cousin with a simple: "Hi."

"Hi," Bojan said. "How are you doing?"

"I'm doing fine."

He waited for his cousin to make the next move, but Bojan seemed to be waiting for him. He knew that Bojan had valuable information about him, which he must have gotten from the two guys, but Bojan didn't know he knew about them, and Milos didn't want to tip his hand, so he only asked: "Have you been thinking about what I said?"

"Yeah. I have," Bojan said, nodding mechanically.

"And did you decide anything?"

"No. But I *did* find out something."

"What did you find out?"

"I found out who told you what happened at that deli."

"Who was it?" Milos asked, glad that he wasn't being taken by surprise.

"It was a girl, a Muslim girl. And according to my sources, you have a relationship with her."

"Yeah, I have a relationship with her."

"Do your parents know about her?"

"My mother does, and she doesn't have a problem with it."

"Maybe she doesn't, but I do. And now I know why you don't want me to get even with those fuckers for breaking my arm."

"That's not the reason. The reason is, I don't want to see what happened in Bosnia happen here."

"It *is* the reason," Bojan growled. "If you weren't screwing this girl, you wouldn't care."

Offended, Milos set the record straight. "I'm not having sex with her, though it's none of your business."

"Whatever you're doing with her, it's my business if it interferes with my getting justice from her family."

"You want them to pay you for breaking your arm?"

Bojan shook his head. "They couldn't ever pay me enough."

"Then what do you want?"

"I want justice."

"No, you don't. You want revenge."

"It's the same thing."

"It's not the same thing. Justice is what's morally right."

"It's morally right for me to get even with them."

"No. It's wrong. It was wrong for them to break your arm, but it's wrong for you to get even with them. And two wrongs don't make a right."

"You have no authority to tell me what's right. You have a personal reason for not wanting me to get even with them."

"If I didn't know this girl, I'd still tell you it's wrong to get even with them."

"If you didn't know her," Bojan said, "we wouldn't be having this conversation. You wouldn't know what happened at that deli. You wouldn't know who I wanted to get even with."

"I'd know it was Muslims. I can read your bumper sticker."

"But they started it. They attacked us."

"Look," Milos said, deciding to try another approach. "I told you that if you get even with them, sooner or later your war with them will hurt our family. But if you don't believe me, think about this. If you get even with them, they'll get even with you, and those guys are members of a gang. They can hurt you more than you can hurt them."

"No, they can't. *My* guys are members of a gang."

"You mean those two guys you were talking with just now in the driveway?"

"Yeah," Bojan said as if he wasn't surprised that they had been observed. "They're members of the toughest gang in Yonkers."

Milos understood. "So you want a war between a gang from Yonkers and a gang from the Bronx?"

"I don't know where his guys are from, I only know they're on the side of the fucking Muslims."

"So that makes a war with them right?"

"Yeah. And it makes a war with Afghanistan right."

"No, it doesn't," Milos said. "It doesn't make either of those wars right. They're both wrong."

Glowering at him, Bojan said: "You don't have the authority to tell me what's wrong."

In a last effort to stop his cousin, Milos said: "Well, before you go any further with your war, just think about what it could do to your parents."

"What could it do to them?" Bojan asked obtusely.

"Ask them. They'll tell you."

Chapter 7

AS SOON AS she had hung up the phone a customer came into the deli with a big order, so Amira didn't have a chance to think about how to deal with the order she had pretended to take on the phone from Milos, and while she was busy serving this customer she forgot about it, until Aunt Malika asked her about it.

"What about that order you took on the phone?"

"Oh, yeah." She realized that she had no choice but to fill the order even though no one would pick it up. She could take it home with her, so it wouldn't go to waste. "I need a grilled chicken on a wedge with lettuce, tomato, and mayonnaise."

Her aunt watched her suspiciously as Amira got a wedge and put it on the cutting board.

"Do you know the person who gave you that order?" Aunt Malika asked.

"I recognized his voice," Amira said.

"It sounded like you did."

She sliced the wedge, wondering if this would be a good time to start trying to get permission to go out at night. If she started with her father he would ask Aunt Malika what she thought, so it would be helpful to prepare her. Willing to risk it, Amira said: "It was the boy I told you about, the one in my religion class."

"You mean the Serb?"

"Yes. And he knows the guy who sprayed our window."

"He does? Does he know him well?"

"He knows him well enough," Amira said, not ready to disclose the fact that the guy was Milos's cousin. "He talked with him, and he tried to make him realize that if he continues his war with us, sooner or later it'll hurt his family.'

"Was he successful?"

"He doesn't know. The guy said he'd think about it."

Aunt Malika considered. "So he's trying to make peace. My heart is with him."

Amira refrained from saying that her heart was with him too.

"What's this boy's name?"

"Milos Stojanović."

"Stojanović. That's a Serbian name. Where does he live?"

"In Yonkers, on Woodland Avenue."

"That's not near here. Isn't there a deli closer to his home?"

"There probably is." She could see where pretending to take an order was going to lead her, especially when he didn't come to pick it up, so she decided to admit the truth. "He didn't call to order a wedge. He called to give me a message."

"So why did you pretend to take an order?"

"Well, I knew you'd ask questions if you heard me talking with someone on the phone."

Aunt Malika smiled at her indulgently. "You could have kept pretending, and I would never have known who it was. But for some reason now you want me to know about him."

"Yeah, I do," Amira said, having stopped making the wedge. "The reason is, I like this boy."

"I could tell from the way you talked with him."

"You could? Really?"

"You're not good at hiding things."

Their conversation was interrupted by a customer who wanted spaghetti and meat balls with garlic bread. While serving him Amira had an idea which as soon as he had gone she tried on Aunt Malika, saying: "If you want to meet him, I could have him come to the store."

"Why not have him come to our house?"

"Because I don't want Hasan to know about him."

"You don't?" Aunt Malika said, looking puzzled. "Why not?"

"Hasan would be jealous."

"Jealous of his cousin?"

"That's how he acts."

"He's just being protective of you. We all are," Aunt Malika admitted, "after what happened to your mother."

"I still don't want Hasan to know about him."

"All right. Have him come to the store."

She didn't pursue the subject further, feeling that for now she had accomplished as much as she could. She would try to have Milos come to the store on Friday after prayers when Aunt Malika would be in a charitable mood.

When she left the store with her father, carrying leftover food as usual, she noticed two guys loitering in the shadows across the street. It made her think of the two guys who had gotten on the bus after her and followed her. Milos's cousin must have sent those guys, and by now he must know that Milos had a Muslim girlfriend. She could only imagine how he would act on that knowledge, and she was glad that she had paved the way for introducing Milos to her family. As soon as her family got to know Milos, and as soon as his family got to know her, they would bless their relationship and stop the war between their cousins.

"In the name of God, the Lord of Mercy," she prayed, "help us to make peace."

She was waiting for her father to lock the door when she spotted Hasan across the street talking with the two guys. It was an opportunity for her to talk with him and try to get him to stop the war, so she told her father: "I need to talk with Hasan about something. You don't have to wait for me."

"How long will it take?" her father asked.

"A while," she said. "And I know you're tired from standing in the kitchen."

"Well, I don't want you to walk home alone."

"Don't worry. I'll get Hasan to walk home with me."

"All right. But don't be long. Your brother will be hungry."

She watched him go, and then she headed across the street directly toward Hasan, who was still talking with the two guys.

The three of them gave her a look that made her feel as if she had no clothes on. She was wearing a headscarf, and confronted by such open male lust she understood why Aunt Malika made her wear one.

"Can we talk?" she asked Hasan, ignoring the two guys.

"Sure," he said obligingly.

She led him down the street far enough so that they could have a private conversation. Then she said: "We don't need those guys to watch the store. The guy who sprayed the window won't come back."

"Why do you think he won't come back?"

"He doesn't want them to break his other arm."

"Well, maybe he'll come back with reinforcements."

"That's what you're hoping, isn't it?"

"No. But if he does, I want to be ready."

"You know," she said, trying to reason with him, "it's not a big deal if he sprays the window. We can clean it off."

"It's a big deal to me," Hasan said stubbornly.

"I don't understand. Can you explain why?"

"The message he sprayed on our window tells me how people feel about us. They hate Muslims. They don't want us here."

"He's only one person. You can't conclude from him how other people feel."

"I'm not concluding it from him," Hasan said. "If most other people didn't feel the same way, this country wouldn't go to war against Muslims."

"It's *not* a war against Muslims," Amira argued. "You heard what the president said."

"Yeah, I heard it. And I don't believe it. If those terrorists had been British, we wouldn't go to war against Britain."

"No, but we'd still try to capture the people who planned the attack, which is all we'll do in Afghanistan."

"You don't think we'll go to war against them?"

"No, I don't think we will, and I pray that we won't."

"Well, we will," Hasan said as if he had inside information. "So you're wasting your time praying that we won't go to war against Afghanistan."

"I have no influence on what our country does, but I do have some influence on what our family does."

"What influence do you have?"

She gathered all her strength to say: "I have the fact that I lost my mother to people who hate Muslims. And I don't hate those people. So why do you hate them?"

"Because they hate us."

"But they didn't do anything to you."

"They sprayed a message on the window of our store."

"You don't have anything to do with the store. You don't work there. You don't do anything to help your father. So why are you so upset by a message that someone sprayed on the window of the store?"

"You don't understand. That message was a warning of more things to come."

"You're reading too much into it."

"No, I'm not" he insisted. "You're not reading enough into it."

"When the guy came back," she explained patiently, "he wasn't doing anything more. He was only spraying the window again."

"Well, if that guy comes back again, he *will* do something more."

"If he does, it's because those guys broke his arm."

Hasan was silent for a while, and then he said: "So what do you expect me to do? Call off my guys and let him come back and do something more?"

"We could ask the police to protect us."

"The police don't care about us."

"I think they do. And from what they said, they don't like it that we hired our own protection. They don't want a gang war in Yonkers."

"We won't have a gang war unless they start one."

"Well, that guy might not come back, but if he does," Amira said, putting her whole self on the line, "I don't want you to hurt him."

"Why not?" Hassan asked, narrowing his eyes. "Why do you care about him?"

"Because he's a human being."

"He's not a human being. He's a Serb."

"He's your brother," she said. "We're children of God."

Hasan snickered. "Where did you get that load of crap? From a Catholic nun?"

"I got it from my mother, who was killed by people like you."

"Your mother wasn't killed by Bosniaks, she was killed by Serbs."

"There's no difference when you're filled with hate. You're all alike. And I'm begging you," she urged him, "to call off those guys and end your war."

"Why do you care if I'm in a war?"

"I don't want anyone to get killed, including you."

"All right," Hasan said after a pause. "I'll think about it."

Since she had made her points she turned to leave, forgetting she had told her father that she would get Hasan to walk home with her.

"Where are you going?" Hasan asked.

"I'm going home."

"Well, I don't want you to walk home alone," Hasan said, sounding like her father. "Could you wait here for a moment? I'll be right with you."

"Okay," she said, submitting to his protection. She watched him return to the two guys and say something to them.

As they were walking home he said: "I called them off. But if that fucking Serb comes back and does anything to damage the store, I'm not going to let him get away with it."

"It's not a big deal if he sprays the window. I'll clean it off."

"If that's all he does, I won't retaliate."

She prayed that he wouldn't come back at all. She repeated the prayer before she went to bed and when she got up the next morning.

Nothing happened to the store that night or the next night, and when she saw Milos in religion class on Wednesday she couldn't wait to tell him the good news. Since there were other students around them in the classroom she could only tell him she had made some progress until they were out in the hallway after class where no one would hear their conversation.

"Guess what," she said happily. "My cousin called off his guys from the Bronx."

"He did? That's great." He put his arm around her shoulder. "So they're not watching the store?"

"No. And nothing has happened to it."

"Thank God. I hope that means my cousin has decided not to get even with him."

"If he only sprays the window," she said, "my cousin said he won't retaliate."

"I'll try again to stop my cousin from doing anything."

Milos walked with her to the classroom where she had her sociology class, and he was outside in the hallway when it was over.

As they walked to the bus stop she said: "I told my aunt about you. I even told her your last name, and it didn't seem to bother her."

"It didn't?" He found her hand and clasped it.

"She wants to meet you, and I told her I'd have you come to the store."

"Okay. When?"

"I think Friday around one would be the best time. It's right after prayers."

"I could make it then. I just have to be at work by two."

"You know," she said after a pause, "when you called me at the store my aunt guessed that I knew the person I was talking with."

"So you didn't fool her by pretending to take an order from someone."

"I probably could have gotten away with it, but I decided to tell her about you. I wanted to get her on our side."

"Have you told your father about me?"

"Not yet. When you come to the store he can meet you then."

"Well, I hope your aunt approves of me."

"Don't worry. She will. Though she still might not let me go out at night," Amira added, not wanting to get his hopes up.

"I understand."

Remembering, she asked: "Did you find out if your cousin sent those guys who followed me?"

"Yeah. He did. He wondered why I was taking such an interest in your store."

"So he knows you have a Muslim girlfriend. Can he use that information against you?"

"No. But it doesn't help my case with him. I mean, he knows I have a personal reason for trying to stop him from having a war with your cousin."

"If you didn't have a personal reason," she asked, believing she knew the answer, "would you still try to stop him?"

"I would," he said without hesitation.

She put her arm around his waist.

Five minutes later she was sitting on her bus, waiting for it to move forward and watching Milos cross the street to where his bus stopped, when she saw two guys behind him. They looked like the guys she had seen Hasan talking with on Monday evening while she waited for her father to lock the store.

Her bus moved forward, and she pressed her face against the window to look back. And then she scrambled to the back of the bus, where she could look through the rear window. The guys were talking with Milos at the bus stop.

She watched them as long as she could, and they were still talking, only talking.

"In the name of God, the Lord of Mercy," Amira prayed. "Please don't let them hurt Milos."

As she rode south toward Getty Square she worried about Milos, and she wondered how she could reach him to make sure he was all right. She decided that the only way was to call the A&P and ask for him.

She assumed that Hasan had sent those guys. She remembered how he had looked at her with narrowed eyes and asked why she cared if he hurt the guy who had sprayed the window. In his jealousy he must have suspected that she had a personal reason for not wanting him to hurt that guy. So he had sent those guys to the college to find out what she was up to, and they would report back to him that she had a boyfriend. Since there were two of them, and they were tough, they could make Milos give them his name, and

Hasan would know that her boyfriend was a Serb with the same last name as the guy who had sprayed their window. If the guy came back and did anything worse to the store, then Hasan would have another reason to get even with him, and his revenge would also have a personal motive.

Filled with apprehension, she got off the bus at McLean Avenue and walked to the deli. She was so preoccupied that she forgot to put on her headscarf before entering, and her aunt gave her a stern look of disapproval, prompting her to take the scarf out of her backpack and wrap it around her hair and under her chin.

"That's better," Aunt Malika said.

"I need to make a phone call," Amira said.

"Go ahead. But don't talk long. We have work to do."

She went to the phone and called information and got the number of the A&P on Nepperhan Avenue. She called the number, and when someone picked up she asked for Milos. It took a long time, but she finally heard his voice: "Hello?"

She thanked God. "Hi. It's Amira. I'm just calling to make sure you're all right."

"You saw those guys at the bus stop?"

"Yeah. And I recognized them."

"Are they the guys who watch your store?"

"Yeah. My cousin must have sent them to check on me."

"Why would he do that?"

"I'll explain later."

"I thought he called them off."

"He did—from watching the store."

"Oh," Milos said. "So now they're watching you?"

"Yeah. Did they find out your name?"

"Well, I either had to tell them or fight them, and there were two of them."

"I understand. It's okay."

"Your cousin's going to guess I'm related to the guy who sprayed your window."

"I can deal with that. Are you still coming to the store on Friday?"

"I'm still planning to. Is there any reason why I shouldn't?"

"No. I'll talk with Hasan before then."

"Well, don't worry. They won't hurt me."

"I'll pray that they won't."

"I love you."

"I love you too," she whispered, hoping it was loud enough for him to hear but not loud enough for her aunt to hear.

When she joined her aunt at the counter she knew she would have to explain the phone call, but she waited for her aunt to ask: "What was that about?"

"You know those guys that Hasan got to watch the store? He sent them to check on me today."

"You mean he sent them to the college?"

"Yeah. When I left the campus with the boy I told you about, they followed us to the bus stop, and they went after him."

"Did they hurt him?"

"No. But they found out his name."

"So? We know he's a Serb."

"He's not only a Serb, but he also has the same last name as the guy who sprayed our window."

"Oh, Lord of Mercy. Are they related?"

"Yeah. They're cousins."

Aunt Malika sighed. "Well, that does complicate things."

"But he's not responsible for what his cousin does."

"You're right. He has no control over what his cousin does."

"He's trying to stop his cousin from getting even with Hasan for breaking his arm. And I got Hasan to call those guys off from watching the store."

"So you're both trying to make peace."

"We want our families to love each other," Amira said, "just as we love each other."

Aunt Malika gazed at her in admiration and then hugged her, saying: "Your mother in heaven is proud of you."

For the first time in her life Amira believed this statement. It strengthened the faith she had in herself, and it helped her summon the courage she needed. "He's coming to the store on Friday so you and Dad can meet him."

"Good. And I'll tell Hasan that he's being too protective. He shouldn't have sent those guys to check on you."

"I'll ask him to call them off."

"I'll tell him to," Aunt Malika said. "He has no authority to have you under surveillance."

"I'm not doing anything wrong. I mean, you know—"

"I believe you. But I don't know this boy or his family, so I have to meet him before I can stop worrying about you."

"When you meet him you *will* stop worrying. He's a nice boy."

Aunt Malika smiled. "You know, when we left Bosnia our people said there was no such thing as a good Serb. But it wasn't always that way. And we were hoping that in America things would be like they were before. You're confirming our hope."

"Hey, ladies, can I get waited on?" a man said good-naturedly.

"Yes, sir," Amira said. "How can I help you?"

"I want a wedge with proshoot, mootzarell, lettuce, and tomato with oil and vinegar."

"You got it." Amira went to get a wedge, feeling better about everything.

That night after dinner Amira went upstairs and rang Uncle Ahmed's door bell. She was glad when Aunt Malika came to the door because she wouldn't have to explain why she wanted to talk with her cousin. She only had to ask: "Is Hasan here?"

"Yes. I'll get him." Her aunt paused. "I talked with him."

"Thanks." She waited outside, not wanting to get into a conversation that might distract her from her mission.

When Hasan appeared he didn't look happy to see her. "What do you want?"

"I want to talk with you. Can we go down to the backyard?"

"My mother already talked with me."

"I still want to talk with you."

His mother was standing not far behind him, so he had no choice. "Okay. But there's nothing you can say that I haven't already heard from my mother."

She led him down the stairs and out to the backyard. It was still warm enough for the crickets to be chirping. A half-moon was shining overhead.

She sat down in one of the chairs at the table where they ate when they cooked outside.

Hasan took one of the other chairs. Before she could say anything he said: "You didn't have to bring my mother into it."

"I'm sorry, but I didn't like being followed by those guys."

"I only did it to protect you."

"You did it to find out if I have a boyfriend."

"I did it to find out if you're involved with the wrong guy."

"You don't have the authority," she said, "to judge whether he's right or wrong."

"Yeah, I do. I'm your blood relative."

"That doesn't give you any authority over me. If you were my father, it would be different."

"Your father doesn't know what's happening. His mind is still in the old country."

"You're the one whose mind is still in the old country. You want to continue the war from there. And now you have another grievance. Your cousin has a Serb boyfriend."

"He's not only a fucking Serb, he's also the brother of the guy who sprayed our window."

"That guy isn't his brother. He's his cousin. And my boyfriend isn't like his cousin. In fact, he's no more like his cousin than I'm like you. So you have no reason to hate him."

"I have a reason," Hasan said. "I know what he wants to do with you."

"You don't know. You only know what *you* want to do."

He glowered at her. "What are you suggesting?"

"You know what I'm suggesting. And if your mother ever saw how you look at me, she'd know what I'm suggesting."

"She wouldn't see anything. God dammit, you're my cousin."

"That's right. And don't forget it."

He looked as if he had finally realized that she was serious. "You actually think I'm jealous of this Serb because I have a thing for you? Well, I don't have a thing for you, and I'm not jealous. I only care what happens to you because you're a member of our family."

"I'm glad you care what happens to me, but you don't have to worry. I'm not with the wrong guy, and I would never do anything to disgrace our family."

"I trust you, but I don't trust your boyfriend."

"Why don't you trust him?"

"Because he's a Serb."

"If you could forget for only a moment that he's a Serb, you might like him. Do you want to meet him?"

"No. I don't," Hasan said, shaking his head.

"Are you afraid you might like him?"

"Why would I be afraid of that?"

"It would contradict your belief about Serbs, and then you'd have to consider them as human beings, instead of something less than human."

Hasan shrugged. "I'm not afraid of that happening."

"Then come to the store on Friday after prayers and you can meet him."

"Maybe I will. And meanwhile," Hasan said after a pause, "I won't have you followed anymore. But I think you should be careful with him. You don't know what guys have in mind when they're with a girl."

Later, as she lay in bed thinking about the conversation, she believed she had moved Hasan in the right direction. But he still had a long way to go because he not only had to stop hating Milos for being a Serb, but he also had to stop being jealous.

Thursday passed without incident, and as soon as she awoke on Friday morning she asked God to make everything go well between Milos and her family when he came to the store for them to meet him that afternoon.

She was having breakfast with her father when the phone rang.

As usual she picked it up because her father had trouble with English over the phone.

It was Uncle Ahmed, who sadly informed her: "I'm at the store, and we have a problem. Last night someone broke the window."

"Oh, no," she moaned.

"There's broken glass everywhere. And whoever did it also made a mess."

"I'm sorry," she said, feeling responsible.

"Could you and your father come over here now and help us clean up?"

"Yeah. Sure." It meant missing prayers, but she thought God would understand. "We'll be there right away."

She returned to the kitchen table and told her father what had happened.

He listened glumly, and then he asked: "Was it the same person who sprayed the window?"

"I don't know, but I think it was."

"It looks like Hasan has gotten us into another war."

"I hope not," she said, but deep down she was afraid they might have reached a point of no return, and she prayed that they hadn't.

They dressed quickly and walked briskly to the store. As they approached it she could see the opening where the window had been, with the "Joe's Deli" sign hanging in the middle. There were shards of glass on the sidewalk, which crunched under their feet as they walked over them and into the store.

Inside, on the floor were cans of soup and boxes of pasta and broken bottles of beer and soda along with the pans for hot food. That was bad enough, but when Amira looked at the board where they wrote the specials of the day she cringed. There were two messages: "Muslims, go home" and "Your daughter is a whore."

"I'm sorry," Aunt Malika said. "I was going to erase that before you got here, but you got here so quickly."

"That's all right. Names can't hurt me."

"Who would write a thing like that?" her father asked.

"A person with a nasty mind," Aunt Malika said.

"They didn't touch the kitchen," Uncle Ahmed said. "Thank God."

"It's my fault," Amira said. "If I hadn't gotten Hasan to call off his guys, this wouldn't have happened."

"Don't blame yourself," her aunt said. "You were trying to make peace. And what if his guys had killed someone?"

"We'd be out of business," Uncle Ahmed said. "And our son would be in jail."

"They didn't do any serious damage," her father said. "We just have to clean up the mess and replace the window."

"I'll pay for the window," Amira said.

"No, you won't," Aunt Malika said. "We needed a new window anyway."

"Yeah, that window came with the store," Uncle Ahmed said. "It must have been more than fifty years old."

"So let's start cleaning up," her father said, bending over to pick up some cans.

They hadn't been working long when Hasan appeared. He looked around the store and at the board where they had sprayed the two messages.

"That fucker!" he roared, unmindful of the women present.

"Watch your language," Uncle Ahmed said.

"You see what happens when I listen to you?" he railed at Amira. "If I hadn't listened to you, this wouldn't have happened."

"What are you talking about?" Uncle Ahmed asked.

"She got me to call off the guys who were watching the store. And you know why she wanted me to call them off? The guy who did this is her boyfriend's cousin."

"Boyfriend?" her father said, surprised. "I didn't know you had a boyfriend."

"We were going to tell you," Aunt Malika said. "In fact, he's coming to the store today so we can meet him."

"If he comes here," Hasan said, "I'll tear him apart."

"No, you won't," Uncle Ahmed said. "We're not going to have any more violence."

"But look what they wrote about your niece."

"It's a standard insult. Your mother's a whore, your sister's a whore, your daughter's a whore. Excuse me, ladies." Uncle Ahmed bowed slightly to the women. "And why do people use such insults?"

"They mean them."

"No. They only want to get a reaction like they got from you."

"Well, I wouldn't react so strongly if there wasn't an element of truth in it."

"What are you saying?" her father asked indignantly.

Hasan faced him. "I'm saying Amira has a boyfriend, a Serb boyfriend, and God only knows what she's doing with him."

"I'm not doing anything wrong."

"That message says you are."

"I'm not. And I know why you're reacting so strongly."

There was a silence.

"Why?" her father finally asked.

"I don't think we need to go into that," Aunt Malika said. "And I agree with Ahmed. There's no basis for what they said about your daughter. It's a standard insult."

"So help us clean up," Uncle Ahmed told Hasan. "And I forbid you from doing anything to get even with them. I don't want any more violence. You hear?"

"Yeah," Hasan mumbled.

With all of them working together it took only about two hours to clean up, and by then Uncle Ahmed had called Store Front Plus about installing a new window. Since it wouldn't be in place until the next day, he called Torre Lumber and asked them to bring some sheets of plywood to cover the opening.

Amira was encouraged by Uncle Ahmed's stand against more violence, but she had doubts about whether Hasan could resist the urge to get even. She even wondered if meeting Milos would help convince him to make peace.

"In the name of God, the Lord of Mercy," Amira prayed, "make everything go well between Milos and my family."

Chapter 8

MILOS GOT OFF the bus and started walking up McLean Avenue, nervous about meeting Amira's family. From what she had told him the main challenge was going to be her Aunt Malika, who evidently made the decisions on what Amira was allowed to do. He wanted to make a good impression, but he didn't know how to present himself other than as he really was, and he hoped her aunt would accept what he was.

His thoughts were disturbed by the sight of a police car ahead of him, parked in front of where he expected the store to be, and he walked faster, dreading that his cousin had done something to get even with them for breaking his arm.

And then he saw the plywood where the window had been.

"Oh, God," he murmured, praying that the store hadn't been wrecked.

When he entered the store he saw two policemen talking across a counter with a man and a woman who he guessed were Amira's uncle and aunt. Not wanting to interrupt the conversation, he held back and waited in front of a case in which there were six-packs of beer. As he looked around he didn't notice any more damage, for which he thanked God.

"So you have no idea who might have done this?" one of the officers was saying.

"No," the man said. "But we think it was the guy who sprayed our window."

"Did he leave any messages this time?"

"He left the same message."

"Then it probably was the same guy," the other officer said.

"Can you think of anyone who might have a grudge against you?"

"No. I can't. I think it's just someone who hates Muslims."

"Okay. Well, if you think of anyone in particular, please let us know. And I'll ask the night patrol to keep an eye on your store."

"Thanks," the man said.

As the police officers walked toward Milos to leave the store he saw Amira standing at the end of the counter. She was wearing a headscarf, so only her face was visible, but if he had seen only her eyes he still would have recognized her.

He immediately moved toward her, saying: "I'm sorry."

"It's all right," she said, moving toward him. "There wasn't much damage."

They stopped with about six inches of space between them.

Then, aware of her uncle and aunt, Milos turned to them and said: "I'm Milos. I'm pleased to meet you. I'm sorry about the damage to your store."

"I'm Ahmed," the man said.

"I'm Malika," the woman said.

"I'll pay for the window," Milos said.

"There's no reason for you to pay for it," Ahmed said.

From a glance at Amira's face he knew she had told her aunt about his relationship to the guy who had sprayed the window and now had broken it, though she evidently hadn't yet told her uncle. "Yes, there is. The guy who did it is my cousin."

"How do you know?"

"He admitted spraying that message on your window."

"Does he have a broken arm?"

"Yes. And I tried to stop him from getting even with your family."

"Well, it looks like he did get even with us. But that should be the end of it. We broke his arm, he broke our window. The arm will heal, and the window will be replaced. So there won't be any lasting damage."

"I still want to pay for the window."

"That's nice of you," Malika said. "But you're not responsible for what your cousin did."

"You're not," Ahmed said. "And we're not going to let you pay for the window."

"Okay," he said. "But I want you to know that my cousin doesn't represent our family. We came here to get away from the hate that caused the war in Bosnia."

"We did too," Malika said. "Tell us about your family."

"Well, there are six of us," he said. "My father, my mother, my grandmother, my two sisters, and me."

"How old are your sisters?"

"Fifteen and sixteen."

"What are their names?"

"Jovana and Tijana."

"Where did you live in Bosnia?"

"In Zenica."

Ahmed shook his head sympathetically. "That wasn't a good situation for Serbs."

"It wasn't, but we're here now. My father and my mother have jobs, my sisters are in high school, and I'm in college, so we're doing all right."

"What are you studying?"

"Physical therapy."

"So you'll help people recover from injuries," Malika said.

"Right. And also from surgeries."

"Well, that sounds like a good career."

"I hope so," he said, feeling more at ease. "I want to be able to help people."

At that point the cook emerged from the kitchen wiping his forehead with a towel.

"Come and meet this nice young man," Malika said, switching from English to Bosnian.

The cook, who had gentle brown eyes and a furry mustache, approached the counter rubbing his palms against his no longer clean white pants.

"Tarik, this is Milos. Milos, this is Amira's father."

"I'm pleased to meet you," Milos said, extending his hand.

Her father shook it, saying: "Likewise. Did you meet my daughter at the college?"

"Yes. We're in the same religion class."

"Milos is studying physical therapy," Malika said.

"Very good," her father said, inspecting Milos as if to make sure that there was nothing wrong with him. "How long will it take you to get a degree?"

"Six years, including this year."

"Who's paying for it?"

"I get financial aid, and I also have a scholarship."

"Amira has a scholarship for getting all A's in high school," Malika said. "She had an almost perfect record."

Amira lowered her eyes modestly.

"What does your father do?" Ahmed asked.

"He's a mechanic. He works in an auto repair shop on Saw Mill River Road. They do a lot of work on transmissions."

"And your mother?" Malika asked.

"She takes care of some rich kids in Irvington."

"How long ago did your family come here?"

"Five years ago. My father and mother still don't speak English very well."

"I don't either," Amira's father said. "It's hard to learn a new language when you're our age."

"I know you young people speak English well," Malika said. "But don't forget your native language."

"I don't think I will," Milos said. "We speak Bosnian at home."

"We do too," Amira said.

"Would you like some coffee or tea or soda?" Malika asked him after a silence.

"No, thanks. I can't stay long. I have to be at work at two-thirty." His supervisor had graciously agreed to let him come to work a half hour late.

"Where do you work?"

"At the A&P on Nepperhan Avenue."

"What do you do?"

"I work at the checkout counter."

"Then you and Amira have similar jobs."

"Except his job probably pays more," Amira joked.

"Are you asking for a raise?" Ahmed teased her.

"I'm sure that Milos's job is more stressful," Malika said. "He has to put up with customers who complain about everything."

"*Our* customers never complain," Ahmed said with a look that revealed they sometimes did.

Milos was gratified by the open way her aunt and uncle were acting in front of him. It made him feel as if they were disposed to accept him.

"Do you work on weekends?" her father asked.

"No. I'm off on weekends."

"So maybe you could come to our house and have dinner with us some weekend."

"That would be great. Thank you." He checked his watch and said: "Well, I better go now. I have to catch my bus. It was nice meeting you."

Almost together her aunt, her uncle, and her father said it was nice meeting him.

"I'll walk you out," Amira said in English.

She followed him out of the store, and they stopped in front of it. The sight of the plywood on the window dismayed him.

"Don't worry about it," Amira told him. "We'll have a new window on Monday. I think you made a good impression on them."

"I hope I did. I like them."

"You'll like my brother Kashir too, and my cousin Rafid."

"What about Hasan?"

"He was here earlier, and he talked about getting even with your cousin. But my uncle told him not to. He said he didn't want any more violence."

"Do you think Hasan listened to him?"

"I don't know. If he won't listen to his father, he won't listen to anyone."

"Well, I'm going to talk with Bojan. What he did to your store is completely unacceptable."

"Maybe you should also talk with his parents."

"Maybe I should. I promised not to tell them why those guys broke his arm as long as he didn't get even with them. But he did, so I'm not bound by my promise anymore."

"I hope he listens to his parents."

He gazed at her beautiful face, which was framed and somehow enhanced by the headscarf. "Are you still free tomorrow?"

"Yeah. Would you like to meet at the library again?"

He thought for a moment. "Could you meet me at the college?"

"That's a good idea," she said with her eyes lighting up. "We could get away from everyone."

"So let's meet at the place where we went that day when we cut our classes."

"Okay. What time?"

"At noon?"

"Okay."

"I love you," he said, overwhelmed by a feeling that made him want to draw her to him and hold her tight.

"I love you too."

They leaned toward each other almost close enough to kiss. But not wanting to risk spoiling the good impression he had made on her family, he held back and only held his palm for her to touch with her palm, which she did, saying: "God be with you."

When he got home after work he found Bojan in the driveway polishing his truck. Of course Bojan could use only his left hand for the job, so it would take longer than usual. But he didn't seem to mind because it was obviously a labor of love.

"Did you get even with them?" Milos asked, getting right to the issue at hand.

"So you heard from your Muslim girlfriend," Bojan said without looking up from his work. He rubbed the surface of the hood as if he was caressing it.

"I saw what you did to their window."

"We could have done more. If you hadn't asked me not to get even, we would have done more. So you should be grateful."

"But if my friend hadn't gotten her cousin to call off the guys who broke your arm, they would have been there, and they might have killed you."

"Well, they weren't there," Bojan said, inspecting the spot that he had been polishing. "And I don't plan to go back again, so I don't have to worry about them."

"You do if they get even with you."

"Just let them try. I'm ready for them."

"You know," Milos said after a pause, "if you paid for the window, they wouldn't have a reason for getting even with you."

"Why should I do that?"

"You broke their window, so you should pay for it."

"They broke my arm, and they didn't pay for it."

"Then you feel you're even?"

"Yeah. I do," Bojan said, turning his attention to another spot.

"When I got to the store," Milos said, changing tactics, "the police were there asking questions. The police asked them if they had any idea who did it. They said they didn't. But they know who did it, and they didn't tell the police."

"They must have been afraid to tell the police."

"They weren't afraid. They were being considerate of me. They know you're my cousin."

Bojan grinned. "Then I guess I don't have to worry about them telling the police."

"Yeah, you do. If I say it's okay, they'll tell the police."

"They can tell the police whatever they want, but they have no evidence."

"Well, I have evidence. You admitted to me that you broke their window."

"Okay. You have evidence. But you wouldn't take *their* side against your family."

"I wouldn't take their side," Milos said, trying to make his position clear. "I'd tell the truth, and being my cousin wouldn't protect you."

Bojan rubbed the hood in silence for a while, and then he said: "If you tell the police I admitted doing it, I'll deny it, and it'll be your word against mine."

"I think the police will believe me."

"Maybe they will. But they might have doubts when they find out that you have a personal interest in the matter."

"I have a personal interest in my family, and if I'm willing to testify against my cousin, they'll know I'm not influenced by personal interests."

"They'll know you don't care about your family."

"You're the one who doesn't care about our family. You're trying to drag us into a war."

"I want justice. And now that we're even," Bojan said, finally looking up from the hood, "I won't do anything more to them."

"Do you promise?"

"I promise. Unless they do something more to me," Bojan added, narrowing his eyes.

"Don't worry. They won't," Milos said with more confidence than he felt. He was counting on Amira's cousin to obey his father.

As he went into the house he wondered if he should tell Bojan's parents what he had done, and he decided it would serve no purpose now that Bojan had promised not to do anything more to Amira's family.

The next morning, after helping his father fix a leaky faucet in the bathroom, Milos took a bus to the college. He had never been there on a Saturday before, and the first thing he noticed was how few cars were in the parking lot. The people whose cars were there today were taking courses at the graduate level in physical therapy, occupational therapy, and physician assistant, and when he finally reached that level in his program he would have courses on Saturday, but today he was free to stroll across the peaceful campus and walk along the path that overlooked the river.

The weather was unseasonably warm, the sky was clear, and the sun was reflecting off the water. A barge was moving slowly upriver, and a power boat was planing in the opposite direction, taking advantage of a perfect day for cruising.

At the end of the path he sat on the bench and gazed across at the Palisades. The leaves on the trees were still mostly green, and they were still bright in the morning sunlight. Later in the morning they would darken in the shadow that fell across the cliff and eventually spread across the river.

Before he even heard or saw Amira he sensed that she was approaching, and he got up and intercepted her. Their bodies collided in a hug, and their mouths came together in a kiss. They swayed in a happy delirium, aware only of each other. They could have been anywhere, but they were especially glad to be here.

"I'm sorry I was late," she said breathlessly.

"You weren't late. I was early."

They found the secluded spot where they had been before, and they sat down there. It wasn't long before they were lying together on the grass, kissing. Since he had no intentions of doing anything beyond that, he put all his heart and mind and soul into it, and he felt her doing the same thing.

"I love you," he said. They were lying on their sides with their faces a few inches apart. He was gazing into her soulful dark eyes and caressing her lush dark hair.

"I love you too."

"I want us to spend our lives together."

"I do too."

"We could get married after we get our bachelor's degrees, and we could live together."

"Yeah, just the two of us."

"With our degrees we could get better jobs than we have now, so we could afford our own apartment."

"I could get a job with the city."

"And I could get a job with a hospital."

"I wish it was already four years from now."

"I do too. But we have to wait until we're married."

"I know. And we will."

They resumed kissing, and they completely lost track of time expressing their love for each other that way.

Then they rolled onto their backs and gazed up at the cloudless sky. He finally felt compelled to say: "I talked with my cousin, and he admitted breaking your window."

"Did you talk with his parents?"

"I decided it wasn't necessary. He promised not to do anything more to your family. I mean unless they get even with him."

"My uncle talked with my cousin again. He told him again not to get even with your cousin."

"What if he doesn't obey his father?"

Amira sighed. "Then I don't know what we're going to do."

"We have to do something. We can't stay out of it."

"Well, maybe," she said after a pause, "we should get them together face to face, so they can both see that their enemy is a human being."

"I like that idea. So where could we get them together?"

"I think the college would be a good place."

"Yeah, it's neutral territory. And maybe we could get Sister Maura to referee them."

"That would be good," Amira said.

"Now, when could we do this?" Milos asked.

"Well, we're all working during the day, so it would have to be an evening or the weekend."

"The weekend might be too long to wait."

"Then how about this Tuesday?"

"I'll ask Bojan."

"And I'll ask Hasan."

They stayed at the spot until the shadow had spread from the Palisades all the way to their side of the river. By then they could feel a hint of fall in the air, so they got up and headed back across the campus. Since they were hungry, they walked to Odell Place and got sandwiches at a deli, which they ate on a bus going south to McLean. They got off there, and after they parted with a kiss he got on a bus that would take him north on Nepperhan, intending to talk with Bojan again at the earliest opportunity.

The truck was gone when Milos got home, and it didn't return until late that evening, so he had to wait until the next day to talk with Bojan. Since it was Sunday, he went in the morning with his father, his mother, his grandmother, and his sisters to St. Mary's, driving over Lake Avenue to North Broadway, all of them packed in one car. St. Mary's was a Russian Orthodox church, but it was the nearest church that was like theirs.

At the end of the service Milos said his own prayer asking God to help him make peace between his cousin and Amira's cousin.

When they got home Uncle Goran was in the backyard lighting a fire in the grill. His mother and Aunt Vidra had planned to take advantage of what might be their last good day for a family cookout, so that was how they would spend the afternoon. At some point Milos would take Bojan aside and talk with him, but first he had to change his clothes and perform his assigned task, which was to help his father clean off the table and chairs. With chairs at each end, the table would seat ten people.

Since they were at home Milos and Pamet were allowed to drink beer, and they stood together in the yard talking while Bojan vacuumed the floor mats of his truck. Aunt Vidra passed him on her way to the grill with the platter of kabobs which she had assembled in the kitchen.

"Come on," she urged her son, "join the party."

"I will," he said. "I'll be done in a minute."

"He loves that truck," Milos said.

"It's like his girlfriend," Pamet said.

They were far enough away so that Bojan couldn't hear them.

"Come to think of it," Milos said, "I've never seen him with a girlfriend."

"Well, I know he's not gay," Pamet said with the authority of someone who was.

"I guess he likes machines more than he likes girls."

"At least he likes something."

Remembering how Pamet had offered to help him, Milos told him what Bojan had done to get even with the guys who had broken his arm.

"Oh, shit," Pamet said, dismayed. "I told him not to get even with them, and I thought he'd listened to me."

"I thought he'd listened to me too."

"So now they'll want to get even with him."

"They will. But my girlfriend and I think we might be able to stop them. The only person in her family who wants a war with our family," Milos explained, "is her cousin Hasan. Her uncle and her aunt, who own the deli, don't want a war. Her father doesn't want a war. And her other cousin doesn't want a war."

"What about her mother?"

"Her mother was killed in Bosnia."

"Aw," Pamet said with sympathy. "The poor girl."

"She was twelve at the time. So she has a reason to hate Serbs, but she doesn't hate us."

"God bless her. Does her cousin have a reason for hating Serbs?"

"His family came here before the war, so he has no particular reason for hating Serbs. He hates us in general."

"The way some people hate gays."

"Or anyone who's different."

Pamet took a deep breath and then exhaled. "If it's only her cousin and Bojan who want a war, then maybe we should put them in a boxing ring."

"That's not a bad idea. At least no one else would get hurt. But if we just have them meet each other, maybe they'll see that the other person is a human being."

"It's worth trying. Have you suggested that to Bojan?"

"Not yet. I'm hoping to talk with him today."

"If you think it would help," Pamet said, "I could join you in that conversation."

"I think it would help. You're his brother, and you're also closer to his age."

"Okay. Let's talk with him after we've eaten. If he's full of food, he'll be more amenable."

As usual the three boys and the two girls ate at one end of the table. Their conversation jumped from one light topic to another, from Jovana's boyfriend, who provided the boys with material for teasing, to Pamet's earring, which his parents weren't happy about. The girls then began a campaign to persuade Bojan to let his hair grow.

"You'd really look cute with hair," Jovana told him.

"I don't want to look cute," Bojan said.

"Well, if you're trying to look scary," Tijana said, "you're succeeding. If I didn't know you, I'd be afraid of you."

"I want people to be afraid of me."

"Why?" Jovana asked.

"So they won't bother me."

"Oh, that's no fun."

This conversation was interrupted by toasts at the other end of the table.

"To our family," Uncle Goran said heartily, raising a shot of *slivovitz*. "May we always stick together no matter what happens."

"To our family," Milos's father said.

"*Za naše dobro zdravlje*," his grandmother said.

While the men downed their shots of *slivovitz*, the women drank from their glasses of wine, and not to be left out, the three boys drank from their bottles of beer and the two girls drank from their bottles of soda.

The girls then got up to help their mother, leaving the boys alone at their end of the table. Bojan was looking very contented.

"You know," Milos said, "we have a way to stop them from getting even with you."

Bojan glanced from him to Pamet. "Are you in on this?"

"Yeah. I am. And I think you should listen to Milos."

"If you just meet with my girlfriend's cousin, he might not want a war with you."

"He might see how tough you are," Pamet said.

"Or he might see what a good guy you are," Milos said, trying very hard to mean it.

"I told you I'm not paying for the window," Bojan said.

"We're not suggesting that," Milos said. "We're only suggesting that you meet with the guy."

Bojan scowled and asked: "Who is he?"

"He's my girlfriend's cousin."

"What's his name?"

"Hasan."

"Hasan," Bojan repeated with a hiss. "That's a Muslim name."

"Of course it is. The guy's a Muslim."

"You want me to meet with a fucking Muslim?"

"I doubt if the guy will be fucking when you meet with him," Pamet quipped.

"I don't see the point of meeting with him," Bojan said.

"The point," Milos explained, "is to stop him from trying to get even with you."

"Well, I don't care if he tries to get even with me. I'm ready for him."

"He could hurt our family," Pamet said. "When you got even with him for breaking your arm, you hurt his family."

"I didn't want to hurt his family," Bojan said, "I only wanted to hurt him."

"If you meet with him," Milos said hopefully, "you might feel differently about him."

Bojan considered. "So what are you proposing?"

"We're proposing that the two of you get together on neutral territory, with a referee who's not from either of our families."

"Do you have anyone in mind?"

"Yeah. One of my teachers."

"That would be okay. But I don't want the police involved."

"The police won't be involved."

"Okay. I'll meet with him," Bojan said, "if he's willing to meet with me. When do you want to have the meeting?"

"How about this Tuesday evening?"

"Okay. I could be available at six thirty."

Milos couldn't wait to tell Amira what he had accomplished with his cousin, and sitting down next to her in religion class, he leaned toward her and whispered: "My cousin agreed to meet with your cousin."

"Mine agreed to meet with yours," she whispered back.

"So let's talk with Sister Maura after the class."

The topic was still Judaism, with emphasis on the Book of Job, which introduced a concept about the relationship between God and man that was different from what the polytheistic religions imagined. In the Book of Job a man questions the arbitrary use of power by an omnipotent God, and even though he can't make God justify his actions he *can* get a response from God, who reminds him of his position in the scheme of things. According to

Sister Maura, the Book of Job paved the way for the individual relationship with God that people had in Judaism, Christianity, and Islam.

"Now, how is that different from polytheism?" Maria asked.

"In most polytheistic religions, the gods are more interested in each other than they are in people—unless they spot an attractive person of the opposite sex." Sister Maura paused for the laughter. "In Judaism God is interested in people, who are His creation. For the first time we get the feeling that God actually cares about His creation and wants people to live up to His expectations."

"If He cared so much about His creation," Steve asked, "then why did He kick Adam and Eve out of the Garden of Eden?"

"Because they disobeyed Him."

"So as long as we obey God, He'll treat us well?"

"But Job obeyed God," Jessica pointed out, "and God didn't treat him well."

"God must be like our parents," Tanya said. "You can obey your parents, but that doesn't mean they'll treat you well."

"If they don't," Eduardo said, "it's not fair."

"That's one thing we learn from the Book of Job," Sister Maura said. "Life isn't always fair, and we have to accept that."

"We have to submit to God's will," Amira said.

"And love Him no matter what happens," Milos said.

"You got it," Sister Maura said, looking at them proudly.

Milos and Amira waited until the other students had left the classroom before they approached Sister Maura.

"Sister," Milos said. "We're hoping you can help us."

Sister Maura looked at them with concern. "Are you in some kind of trouble?"

"We're not, but our families are. I mean two members of our families."

"We're from Bosnia," Amira said. "My family is Bosniak, his family is Serb, and where we came from Bosniaks and Serbs hate each other."

"I understand," Sister Maura said. "Did they bring that feeling here with them?"

"No. they didn't," Milos said. "It's one of my cousins and one of her cousins who hate each other. And they have no reason to hate each other. They didn't live there during the war."

"Unfortunately," Sister Maura said, "people don't always need a reason to hate each other."

"But they don't even know each other."

"That's where we're hoping you can help us," Amira said. "We got our cousins to agree to meet with each other, but we need a neutral referee."

"Where would this happen?"

"Here, at the college."

"You believe that if your cousins meet with each other, face to face, they'll stop hating each other?"

"We hope they will."

Sister Maura nodded, looking at them benignly. "So you want to make peace."

"We do," Milos said. "We want to make peace for our families and for the whole world."

"So when is the meeting?"

"It's this Tuesday at six-thirty."

"Okay. I'll do it. How many are coming?"

"Amira and me and our two cousins."

"Then we can use my office."

"Thank you so much," Amira said.

"Thank you," Milos said.

"Blessed are the peacemakers," Sister Maura said, looking at them with admiration.

As usual Milos met Amira after their next class, and they walked together to the bus stop. They felt their effort to make peace between their cousins was going well, and they were grateful to Sister Maura for being willing to help them. They realized that anything could happen at the meeting, good or bad, but they were optimistic. Just getting their cousins to agree to meet with each other was a major accomplishment.

When her bus appeared in the distance they kissed each other goodbye: once, twice, and a third time for good luck. And watching the bus take her away, Milos felt as if his heart was being pulled out of him.

After standing there a while he crossed the street and started waiting for his bus. Almost immediately he became aware of two guys who emerged from behind the stone wall that enclosed the property across from the college. They were the guys who had made him tell them his name, and they looked as if they wanted something more from him.

They both had shaved heads, they were both wearing black tee shirts over tight black jeans, and they both had tattoos on their forearms.

"I guess you didn't get our message," the big guy said.

"Uh, what was your message?"

"To stop seeing that girl."

"Why should I stop seeing her?"

"We told you why," the wiry guy said emphatically. "She's the cousin of the guy we work for, and he doesn't want you screwing his cousin."

"I'm not screwing her."

"We saw you kissing her."

"There's no law against kissing."

"Maybe there isn't, but there's a penalty for not doing what we tell you."

"What is it?" Milos asked, already guessing.

"This," the big guy said, punching him in the stomach.

Milos was expecting it, so it didn't hurt him as much as it could have, but it was followed by a blow to his head that made him see stars.

He drew back, preparing to defend himself.

"I assume you know what we did to your cousin," the wiry guy told him.

"Yeah. I know. You broke his arm."

"Well, we could break both your arms."

"And both your legs," the big guy added.

"This time we won't hurt you," the wiry guy said as if they were doing him a tremendous favor. "But next time we will if you don't get the message."

"I got the message," Milos said.

"Then next time that girl comes to the bus stop," the big guy said, "we don't want to see you with her. You understand?"

"I understand. But I have a question."

"What's your question?"

"Why are you doing this?"

"Her cousin asked us to defend the honor of his family."

"But how will it defend the honor of his family if you stop me from seeing her?"

"It'll stop you from getting her pregnant," the wiry guy said.

"You need to study biology," Milos told him. "Girls don't get pregnant from kissing."

"Kissing leads to other things," the big guy said, sounding just like his grandmother giving a lecture to his sisters.

"Why do you care about the honor of his family?"

"We don't," the wiry guy said. "But we care about the honor of our gang."

"The honor of your gang? I don't get it."

"We agreed to do a job for Hasan," the big guy said, "and we always keep our agreements."

"But it's gotten you into a war between Bosniaks and Serbs."

"Oh, we're not in that phony war. We're in a *real* war with a gang in Yonkers."

"A gang in Yonkers?"

"The guys your cousin got to trash that store. Who do you think they are?"

"I have no idea," Milos said, beginning to see the absurdity of the situation. "You mean this is a war between gangs?"

"Yeah, you got it," the wiry guy said.

"But don't you see how Hasan is using you?"

"No, how is he using us?"

"He's jealous of his cousin," Milos said, "and he's using you to stop her from seeing me. But it's not just me. He wants to stop her from seeing any guy."

"How can he be jealous of her. People don't feel that way about their cousins."

"Hasan does. He lusts for her."

"That's perverted," the big guy said with righteous indignation.

"Well, that's why Hasan had you follow her," Milos told them, spotting his bus in the distance. "He has a thing for her."

"I know what you're doing," the wiry guy said. "You're trying to talk your way out of this. But it won't work."

"And when Hasan hears what we saw you doing with her," the big guy said, "you're going to be in trouble."

Milos felt an urge to ask them not to tell Hasan what they had seen, but he realized that his plea would only make them more eager to tell him.

Before he got on the bus he reminded them: "Hasan is using you for his own purpose."

Riding down Executive Boulevard, he worried that instead of being a reason for peace between their families, the love between him and Amira might end up being a pretext for war, and he wondered what to do about Hasan's jealousy.

When he got to the A&P he went to the pay phone and called Amira and told her about his encounter at the bus stop.

"Did they hurt you?" she asked, sounding concerned.

"No. But they told me to stop seeing you."

"Hasan has no authority to do that."

"Well, I'm not going to stop seeing you."

"But I don't want those guys to hurt you. I'll have to talk with Hasan."

"They've probably told him what they saw, so be prepared."

"I will be. I'm going to tell my aunt what happened. I think she should know that Hasan sent those guys to threaten you."

"Yeah, tell her what happened," Milos said. "We need all the help we can get."

As he lay awake in bed that night he veered back and forth between the hope that everything would go well at the meeting the next day and the fear that Hasan's jealousy would upset the delicate balance of the situation.

Around five in the morning he was awakened by a scream that could have come from someone discovering the dead body of a loved one. Sitting up in bed, he realized that the scream had come from the driveway, and hearing it again, he recognized the voice of Bojan, crying out in agony.

Milos pulled on his jeans and raced barefoot downstairs and out the back door.

He found Bojan standing in front of his truck, still in the tee shirt and shorts he had slept in, making a gesture with his hands as if he was grasping a rope in each of them. There were no apparent wounds on his body, but the windshield of his truck was broken, and there was a message carved in the shiny surface of the hood, which said: "Serbs, go home."

Chapter 9

THAT MORNING AMIRA got a ride to the college with her cousin Rafid, who had bought an old car during the summer with the money he had saved from his job as a waiter. Rafid had classes on Tuesdays and Thursdays that started at the same time as hers, so on those days she didn't have to take the bus in the morning.

"When am I going to meet your boyfriend?" Rafid asked as they drove through Getty Square.

"You could meet him on a day when the three of us have classes," Amira said, wondering if her whole life would be as constrained by schedules as it was now.

"What's his major?"

"Physical therapy."

"So he's taking biology, anatomy, and physics? Those are tough courses."

"Yeah, they are. I don't know if I could pass them."

"Of course you could. You're good at math, and that helps in science, doesn't it?"

"Yeah. But I didn't do well in calculus."

"You mean you got an A minus instead of an A?"

In fact, she had. It had been her lowest grade in senior year. "Well, luckily I don't have to take those courses."

They stopped for the light at Ashburton Avenue. "So have you made any progress in stopping the war between my brother and your boyfriend's cousin?"

"I think we have. At least I got your brother to agree to meet with my boyfriend's cousin."

"When are they meeting?"

"This evening."

"Where?" Rafid edged the car forward in anticipation of the light changing.

"At the college, in the office of our religion professor."

"Who's your professor?"

"Sister Maura."

"I had her for that course. And you know what? I learned more from her about our religion than I did from my parents."

"We're still studying Judaism, but I'm hoping to learn more about Christianity."

The light changed, and Rafid stepped on the accelerator, saying: "I don't understand why people make such a big deal about religious differences. After taking that course I know there aren't any major differences. But the people who sell religions want us to believe there *are* major differences. They're like the people who sell Coke and Pepsi, who want us to believe there's a major difference, but can you tell the difference?"

"No, I can't. But some people can."

"They pretend they can because they believe the marketing. They've been brainwashed into believing there's a difference."

"If there are no differences, then why do we have Judaism, Christianity, and Islam?"

"For the same reason we have Coke and Pepsi—competition for market share."

Amira could see how majoring in marketing had influenced her cousin's view of the world. "But they don't compete in the same way. I mean, Coke and Pepsi don't kill people in their wars."

"Religions don't either. They're used as a pretext for wars. Like the war against Islam that our country's about to start. It's not about Islam, it's about oil."

"Do they have oil in Afghanistan?"

"No. But that's where they can most easily get away with starting the war."

"Do you think the war will spread from there?"

"I think it will. There's nothing in Afghanistan that our country wants, except Osama bin Laden. And if they don't get him," Rafid added, "they'll have a pretext for expanding the war."

Amira reflected. "So what's the war between Hasan and my boyfriend's cousin about?"

"That's a good question. I don't know your boyfriend's cousin, but I know Hasan, and for him it's not religion, it's hate."

"I think it is. But where does the hate in Hasan come from?"

"It might just be in him. And it needs an object, so with our family history it's logical for him to hate Serbs."

"But he didn't know that the guy who sprayed our window was a Serb. He only found out after they broke his arm."

"You're right. If the guy had been black, he might have wanted a war against blacks. But he was primed for a war against Serbs."

"If he was," she said, "then it doesn't help that my boyfriend is a Serb, or that the guy who broke our window is my boyfriend's cousin."

"If my brother didn't want a war, he wouldn't care what your boyfriend was."

"Well, he still wouldn't want me to have a boyfriend."

"What do you mean?"

"I think your brother is jealous of Milos."

Rafid slowed the car as they approached the light at Shonnard Place. "I've noticed how Hasan looks at you, and how he protects you, so he could be jealous. But that shouldn't stop you from having a boyfriend."

"I know it shouldn't. But it makes me feel responsible for this war."

"You're not responsible for it," Rafid told her definitely. "Hasan is responsible. When your boyfriend's cousin sprayed the window of our store, Hasan didn't have to get even. But he did get even, so he's responsible for our window being broken. And I hope you can stop him from getting even now."

"I do too," she said, appreciating Rafid's support.

Amira had trouble concentrating in her English class because she kept thinking about the meeting between Hasan and Bojan that would take place that evening. When she had awakened in the morning she had prayed that everything would go well, and now in class she prayed again: "In the name of God, the Lord of Mercy, please make everything go well in the meeting. Make each of them see that the other person is a human being."

"Amira," the professor said, "could you tell us why the author included this scene?"

"I'm sorry," she said. "I wasn't following the discussion."

The professor, a woman in her late twenties who had very high expectations, must have detected that she wasn't paying attention and called on her purposely. "I guess you have something more important on your mind."

"I'm sorry. I didn't mean any disrespect."

"Well, pay attention. You can't learn if you're not present." The professor then called on another student, and at least for a while Amira didn't think about the meeting.

When she left the classroom she found Milos waiting for her, and she could tell from his face that something had happened.

"We need to talk," he said. "Can you cut your next class?"

"Sure." It was history, her easiest course.

Without having to say anything further they left the building and headed for the path that overlooked the river. As soon as they were beyond the range in which anyone could hear their conversation, Milos said: "Hasan got even with Bojan."

"Oh, no," she said with crashing hopes. "What did he do?"

"He broke the windshield on Bojan's truck, and he carved a message on the hood that said 'Serbs, go home.' I don't think he did it himself," Milos added. "I think he had his guys from the Bronx do it."

"So Bojan won't meet with Hasan now?"

"I doubt if he will. He's furious. He cares more about that truck than anything."

Amira tried to understand her cousin's motivation. "I think I know why Hasan did it. I think he did it because those guys told him they saw us kissing."

"If he's jealous of me, why didn't he have them do something to me?"

"Well, he wanted to get even with Bojan anyway, and that gave him another reason."

"I guess that makes sense. And by doing what he did to Bojan, he made sure I got his message to stop seeing you."

"He has no authority to tell you to stop seeing me."

"He thinks he does."

"But he doesn't," she maintained. "And he has no authority to make me feel what he did to your cousin's truck is my fault."

Milos stopped and faced her. "Is that how you feel?"

Trying to hold back the tears, she said: "Yeah. That's how I feel."

"It's not your fault that your cousin's jealous of you. That's his problem."

"But I gave him a reason to be jealous."

"So you're not allowed to have a boyfriend?"

"I'm not saying that. I'm only saying that if those guys hadn't seen us kissing, Hasan might not have done anything."

"It's not your fault that we were kissing. I kissed you."

"I let you kiss me, and I kissed you back."

He gestured helplessly. "We shouldn't blame ourselves for kissing. We were only expressing our love for each other."

"I know. But maybe we shouldn't have been kissing in public," she added, knowing what her aunt would have thought about it.

"Please don't blame yourself. Your family didn't start this war. My family did. My cousin sprayed that message on the window of your uncle's store. And when your cousin got even with my cousin, he didn't know about your relationship with me. So we're not responsible for our cousins being at war with each other."

"You're right," she said, feeling a little better. "But I still feel responsible for not being able to stop their war."

"I do too," he admitted.

"Since we love each other we *should* be able to stop their war."

"Well, maybe we still can. But we have to stop Bojan from getting even with Hasan now. He loves that truck, so Hasan hit him where it really hurts."

"I'm sorry," Amira said, reaching out to him.

He put his arms around her and hugged her, and that made her feel much better.

They continued walking, crossing over the stone bridge, and

going to their secluded spot. The river was peaceful, and the Palisades were illumined by the morning sun. There was still a haze blurring the skyline of the city, so they couldn't see that the twin towers were now missing.

They sat down on the grass facing the Palisades.

"Sometimes I wish," Milos said dreamily, "we could get into a boat and float down the river and get away from everyone."

"I do too," she said, gazing across the water.

"Where would we go?"

"Where we could make a new world."

Milos sighed. "That's what people thought they were doing when they came here."

"From what I can see, they didn't make this world any better than the old world."

"That's because they brought their problems with them."

"I hope we wouldn't do the same thing."

"I do too. But maybe we *would* do the same thing, so we shouldn't judge them. We should just try to do better."

"Yeah."

They were silent for a while, and then he said: "But we can't get into a boat and float down the river and get away. We have to deal with this situation."

"I'll pay for the damage to Bojan's truck," Amira offered.

"You shouldn't pay for it. I should pay for it."

"Why should you pay for it?"

"My cousin broke the window in your store, and your cousin was only getting even with him for doing that."

"It wasn't only that," she said. "My cousin had another reason."

"Whatever his reasons, he should feel they're even now. But now it's *my* cousin who wants to get even."

After a pause Amira said: "Do you think it would help if Hasan offered to pay for the damage?"

"I think it might. Would Hasan be willing to do that?"

"I don't know," she said, wondering if he would. "If I tell his parents what he did, they should be able to make him do it."

"Bojan would have to be willing to accept payment for the

damage. He wouldn't have to forgive your cousin, but he *would* have to make peace with him."

"So we have to get them to meet with each other before your cousin does anything more."

"I have an idea," Milos said tentatively. "I could tell Bojan's parents that your cousin is willing to pay for the damage, and you could tell Hasan's parents that my cousin is willing to accept payment for the damage. We don't know if they *are* willing, but if they both think the other is willing, then maybe we can get them to meet with each other."

She didn't see anything wrong in that approach. They wouldn't exactly be lying because they didn't know that their cousins weren't willing, and they would be doing the right thing by trying to get their cousins to make peace. "Okay. But I think we should move the meeting to tomorrow so we have time to talk to their parents."

"We need to ask Sister Maura if she can do it then."

"Should we try to find her now?"

"Yeah. I think we should."

They got up and walked across the campus to the building where the faculty of liberal arts had their offices. Luckily, they found Sister Maura in her office, correcting papers. She looked up and smiled as if she was glad to see them.

"Is our meeting still on?" she asked them.

"Well, that's what we came to ask you about," Milos said. "We wondered if you could do it tomorrow at the same time."

Sister Maura checked the calendar on her desk and said: "Yes. I can. But I have an event at seven-thirty."

"That should give us enough time."

"Then I'll put it in my calendar." Sister Maura made a note and then said: "I have a feeling that something happened."

"Something did happen," Amira said. "My cousin got even with his cousin."

"Lord, have mercy. I hope he didn't hurt him."

"He only damaged my cousin's truck," Milos said. "But my cousin cares more about that truck than anything. So he's furious, and he wants to get even."

"An eye for an eye," Sister Maura said, "until the whole world is blind."

"We want to stop him from doing anything," Milos continued. "So I'm going to tell my cousin's parents that Amira's cousin is willing to pay for the damage, and Amira's going to tell her cousin's parents that my cousin is willing to accept payment for the damage. And we're hoping that will bring them together."

"Are they both willing?"

"We don't know," Amira said. "But we're hoping they are, so it's not wrong to tell each one of them separately that the other is willing, is it?"

"No. You're trying to stop them from hurting each other."

"We should know if they're willing," Milos said, "by the time we see you in class tomorrow. Is that okay?"

"It's fine," Sister Maura said. "God be with you."

"Thank you, sister," Milos and Amira said, almost at the same time.

Amira was dutifully wearing her headscarf when she entered the deli just before two, and she was greeted by an approving look from Aunt Malika, who didn't have to say: "Your mother in heaven is proud of you."

At the moment there were no customers, so Amira took advantage of the opportunity to prepare Aunt Malika for the talk she wanted to have that evening. She quickly told her aunt what Hasan had done to get even with Milos's cousin for breaking the window in their store, and she voiced her concern that now his cousin would get even with Hasan.

"It sounds like the war in Bosnia," her aunt said sadly.

"It does, but we're hoping we can bring them together and make peace."

"You say you're hoping, but do you have any reason to believe you can bring them together?"

"Well, Milos's cousin is willing to accept payment for the damage, so we only have to get Hasan to pay for the damage."

"How much will it cost to repair the truck?"

"I don't know. But his cousin's father owns a repair shop, so that should help."

"It should," Aunt Malika said. "They could do the job at cost."

"So I'm asking if you and Uncle Ahmed and I can have a talk with Hasan tonight. I want him to agree to pay for the damage and to meet with Milos's cousin."

"Where would you have them meet?"

"At the college. Our religion professor has agreed to referee the meeting. She's a Catholic nun, so she's impartial."

Her aunt frowned. "The Catholics weren't impartial in Bosnia, but they were mostly on our side because we were the enemy of their enemy. I hope this nun isn't a Croat."

"No. She isn't. I think she's Irish."

After a pause Aunt Malika asked: "What do you think Milos's cousin would do to get even?"

"I don't know, but I'm afraid it would be something worse than what Hasan did to him."

"So we better have that talk with Hasan and get him to meet with Milos's cousin before he does something worse. I'll call you this evening after we've had dinner. You should bring your father," her aunt added.

"Okay," she said, seeing no way to avoid involving her father in the situation, though she would have liked to spare him.

After her aunt and uncle left she looked for an opportunity to talk with her father, but she didn't have one until they were walking home. She told him what Hasan had done, and she explained how she was trying to prevent the war from escalating any further.

Her father listened, and then he asked: "The boy who came to the store last Friday, why is he involved in this situation?"

"The guy who broke our window is his cousin."

"His cousin? So which side is he on?"

"He's on my side," Amira said. "And I'm on the side of peace."

"Then I'm on your side," her father said. "I had enough war in Bosnia."

They had just finished eating their dinner of leftover beef stew from the deli when her aunt called and invited them to come upstairs.

They found her uncle and aunt and Hasan sitting in the living room, looking tense.

"Hi, princess," Uncle Ahmed said in the usual way. "*Dobro veče, Tarik.*"

"*Dobro veče,*" her father said.

"Come and sit with me," Aunt Malika said, moving over so there was a place beside her on the sofa.

Amira joined her aunt on the sofa, and her father took the remaining chair.

"Tarik, did your daughter tell you what's going on?"

"She told me enough," her father said.

"Please tell us what you told your aunt," Uncle Ahmed said gently.

"Hasan broke the windshield of Bojan's truck—"

"Explain to us who Bojan is."

"He's Milos's cousin."

"Milos is the boy you met at the store," her aunt reminded her father.

"I remember him," her father said. "He seemed like a nice boy."

"Hasan also carved a message in the hood of the truck," Amira continued.

"What did the message say?" Uncle Ahmed asked.

"It said 'Serbs, go home.'"

"I didn't touch that truck," Hasan said, glaring at her.

"If you didn't do it," Amira said, "then your guys from the Bronx did it."

"Well, I didn't tell to them to do it."

"Then why did they do it?'

"To get even with him."

"For breaking the window in our store?"

"Tell us the truth," Uncle Ahmed said sternly. "Did you tell those guys to do it?"

Hasan squirmed. "All right. I did. But he broke our window."

"I told you not to get even with him," Uncle Ahmed reminded him, more angry that she had ever seen him. "I told you I didn't want any more violence. And you disobeyed me."

"I wanted justice."

"You didn't want justice. You wanted revenge."

"I also wanted to defend the honor of your daughter," Hasan said to her father.

"You mean because of that message he left?" her father asked.

"I told you," Uncle Ahmed said, "it was a standard insult. He only wrote it to get a reaction. And it looks like he did."

"In any case," Amira told Hasan, "you had no reason to defend my honor. I haven't done anything to dishonor our family."

Hasan looked as if he was about to disagree, but he evidently changed his mind. He said to his father: "So you don't care what he did to our store?"

"Yes, I care. I put the past ten years of my life into that store. But I could have lived with him spraying messages on the window. We only had to clean them off. And I could have lived with him breaking the window and trashing the store. We only had to replace the glass and clean up the mess. But now you've gone and damaged his truck. Did you ever think about what he might do to get even with us?"

"Don't worry. I'm ready for him."

"You're not ready for anything, and you're not going to continue this war. You're going to meet with Bojan, and you're going to pay him for the damage. You hear?"

"Yeah," Hasan mumbled.

"If you disobey me again," Uncle Ahmed warned him, "I'm going to disown you. I'm not going to recognize you as my son. You hear?"

"Yeah."

In bed that night she said another prayer, and believing that Milos could get his cousin to agree to a meeting, she fell asleep.

She was suddenly awakened at three-thirty in the morning by a commotion upstairs. She heard the footsteps of people running around and the voices of her uncle, her aunt, and Hasan. She got up and quickly dressed and went outside, where she encountered Uncle Ahmed and Aunt Malika.

"What happened?" she asked anxiously.

"The police called," Uncle Ahmed told her. "Someone torched our store."

"Oh, God," she moaned, feeling it was her fault.

Her father immediately joined them and learned what had happened. Her uncle and aunt were going to the store, so Amira and her father went in the car with them. Sitting behind her uncle, Amira put on her headscarf in response to a backward glance from her aunt.

When they turned into McLean she could see a fire engine ahead of them in front of the store. There was also a police car with flashing lights.

Unable to park on McLean, they went into a side street and left the car there. As soon as she got out Amira could smell the smoke, and fearfully she prayed: "In the name of God, the Lord of Mercy, please don't let anyone be harmed."

Reaching McLean, she saw the blackened front of the store, and her eyes went up to the floors above where people lived in apartments. The windows were intact, and there were no outward signs of damage. The tenants, whom she recognized, were standing on the sidewalk, looking unhappy but unharmed.

In front of the store were two policemen, the ones who had responded to the broken window, and Uncle Ahmed went to them, asking: "Is the fire out?"

"Yeah. It's out," the tall officer said. "And we got everyone out of the building."

"Thank God for that," Uncle Ahmed said as if it was his main concern.

"Except for the smoke, there wasn't any damage to the upper floors, and there wasn't any damage to the structure of the building, but there was a lot of damage to your store, not only from the fire but also from the water."

"I can see that," Uncle Ahmed said, peering through the open space where the new window had been. "But it could have been worse."

"It could have been," the hefty officer said. "Luckily, one of the tenants woke up and heard them fighting on the sidewalk and called nine-one-one."

"Fighting on the sidewalk?"

Following the direction of her uncle's eyes, Amira noticed blood stains on the area of the sidewalk that was cordoned off with yellow tape.

"Whoever you had watching the store," the tall officer said, "must have tried to stop whoever set the fire, and at least one guy was wounded."

"Was anyone here when you arrived?" Uncle Ahmed asked.

"No. They were all gone."

Her uncle shook his head sadly.

"When did the tenant call you?" Aunt Malika asked.

"At quarter of three," the hefty officer said.

"Then the firemen must have gotten here quickly," Uncle Ahmed said.

"They were here within fifteen minutes."

"Do you have any idea who might have done this?" the tall officer asked her uncle.

Uncle Ahmed hesitated.

"You know, when your window was broken I had a feeling you knew more than you told me, and now I think you better come clean."

Uncle Ahmed looked at Amira as if he needed her permission. She nodded, wishing they had gone to the police earlier.

"We think it was the cousin of our niece's boyfriend," Uncle Ahmed said. "But if it was, he did it to get even with our son."

"What did your son do to him?"

"He damaged his truck. But that was to get even with him for breaking our window, which the cousin of our niece's boyfriend did to get even with our son for breaking his arm."

"How far back does this go?" the hefty officer asked.

"To Bosnia," Uncle Ahmed said.

"Bosnia? What do you mean?"

"We're Bosniaks, and they're Serbs."

"Oh, yeah," the tall officer said. "You had a war there."

"We came here to get away from it. But our son and the cousin of our niece's boyfriend are continuing it here."

"Are you the niece?" the tall officer asked her.

"Yes," she said, lowering her eyes.

"What's your name?"

"Amira Hasanić."

"Could you spell that for me?" the officer asked, taking out a notebook.

She did, softly but clearly. And in response to his questions she gave him the names of her boyfriend and his cousin.

"Do you know where Bojan lives?"

"Yeah. He lives in the same house as Milos." She gave him the address on Woodland Avenue.

"Thank you," the tall officer said gently, and then to Uncle Ahmed: "I understand that your son has some guys watching the store at night. Do you know who they are?"

"No. I only know they're from the Bronx."

"Do you know if they're members of a gang?"

"No, but I wouldn't be surprised if they are. We've never been happy with the guys our son hangs out with."

The officer turned to her and said: "If Bojan did this, he wasn't alone. He must have had some guys with him."

"He must have," she agreed. "He had two guys follow me."

"He had them follow you?" Aunt Malika said. "Why?"

"To find out who Milos was seeing. But Hasan had two guys follow me," she added, "to find out who I was seeing."

"It sounds like they were making an issue of your relationship," the tall officer said.

"They were," she said. "But *we* weren't the cause of their war. It started before either of them knew we had a relationship."

"Then maybe they were trying to drag you into it."

"They never could have done that. We were trying to make peace between them."

"They were," Uncle Ahmed confirmed. "In fact, they arranged for Hassan to meet with Bojan this evening."

"Well, it's too bad Bojan couldn't wait," the hefty officer said, looking at what was left of the store.

"We're going to talk with Bojan now," the tall officer said, closing his notebook. "If we find evidence that he torched your store, we're going to charge him with arson. And if we find evidence that Hasan damaged Bojan's truck, we're going to charge him with vandalism. But judging from those blood stains on the sidewalk, I think we have more than a war between Hasan and Bojan. I think we have a war between two gangs."

A few minutes after the policemen left, Hasan appeared with Rafid behind him. It was as if Hasan had been waiting for the police to go before he came onto the scene.

"Shit," he said in awe, looking at the store.

"Are you surprised?" Uncle Ahmed asked bitterly.

"Yeah. I am. How could they have done this?"

"You weren't here last night?"

"Why would I be here? I had those guys watching the store."

"Well, they didn't do a very good job of watching it."

"They must have been outnumbered."

"You said you were ready for him, but you weren't ready. You underestimated your enemy. And look what they did to us."

"You have insurance."

"Our insurance won't cover everything. And until we rebuild the store, your mother and I won't have any income. Your uncle won't have a job. Your cousin won't have a job."

"It's not my fault."

"It *is* your fault," Uncle Ahmed roared. "I told you not to get even with them for breaking our window, and you disobeyed me."

"I only did it because of her," Hasan said, pointing to her.

"What do you mean?"

"You remember the message they left when they broke the window?"

"Yes. It said: 'Muslims, go home.' "

"It also said: 'Your daughter is a whore.' "

"I told you, that's a standard message. It has no basis."

"It does have a basis," Hasan said. "My guys saw her having sex with that Serb."

"They saw us kissing. That's all."

"You were kissing Milos?" Aunt Malika said, shocked.

"There's nothing wrong with kissing. It's a way of expressing friendship and love."

"You weren't just kissing. They saw you having sex with him."

"I don't believe it," her father said. "She's a good girl."

"I'm only telling you what my guys saw."

"Well, I don't believe it," her father repeated.

"What really happened is," she said, "he had two guys follow us, and they saw us kissing. And when they reported it he was jealous. So he went and damaged Bojan's truck."

"I didn't do it out of jealousy. I did it to defend the honor of our family."

"Whatever your reason," Uncle Ahmed said, "you disobeyed me, and you're responsible for what they did. Don't try to blame Amira."

"So you don't care if she dishonors our family?"

"I didn't dishonor our family. You did, with your hate."

"Amira's right," her aunt said. "Your hate is going to ruin us."

"Amira isn't responsible for what they did," her father said, supporting her firmly. "*You* are responsible."

Hasan was silent, with lowered eyes.

"Now, listen," Uncle Ahmed said, delivering an ultimatum. "If you do anything to get even with them, I'm not only going to disown you, I'm also going to report you to the police. I'm going to testify against you, my own son, and I'm going to see that they lock you up. You hear?"

"Yeah," Hasan mumbled.

Amira appreciated the support from her uncle, her aunt, and her father, but gazing at the wreckage of the store, she still felt it was her fault. And she wondered if her mother in heaven was proud of her.

Chapter 10

WHEN HE FINALLY fell asleep that night Milos was feeling almost positive about the situation. He had gone downstairs after dinner and met with Uncle Goran, Aunt Vidra, and Bojan to convey the offer from Hasan to pay for the damage to the truck. He didn't know if there was such an offer, but he believed that Amira would get it.

He found his uncle and aunt at the dinner table, having coffee.

"Is Bojan here?" he asked, afraid that he might have come too late.

"He's in his room," Aunt Vidra said. "Would you like to talk with him?"

"I'd like to talk with the three of you."

"What about?" Uncle Goran asked.

He got to the point. "The guy who damaged Bojan's truck is willing to pay for it."

"You *know* this person?" Aunt Vidra asked indignantly.

"I don't actually know him," Milos said. "I know his family, and I'm trying to make peace between him and Bojan."

"Why don't you sit down," Uncle Goran suggested. "Would you like a coffee?"

"No, thank you." Milos sat down in an empty chair. The dinner table had a round glass top, and there were four orange placemats on it.

"Now, tell us what's happening."

"Could you ask Bojan to join us? I don't want to talk behind his back."

"Bojan?" Uncle Goran shouted. "Come here."

Within a few minutes Bojan appeared, looking surprised to see him at the table. His eyes asked: "What the hell are you doing here?"

"Sit down," Uncle Goran said. "Milos has something to tell us."

Bojan reluctantly sat down in the chair opposite Milos.

"Repeat what you said about the guy who damaged Bojan's truck."

"He's willing to pay for it," Milos said, looking at his cousin.

"How do you know?" Bojan asked gruffly.

"You know how I know."

"Wait a minute," Uncle Goran said to him. "Is there something you're not telling us?"

"What he's not telling you," Bojan said, "is that he has a Muslim girlfriend, and it's her cousin who wrecked my truck."

"You have a Muslim girlfriend?" Aunt Vidra asked, shocked.

"We all had Muslim friends before the war," Uncle Goran reminded her.

"She's a student at the college," Milos said, though he felt he shouldn't have to explain.

"Did she tell you her cousin's willing to pay for the damage?" Uncle Goran asked.

"Yes. She talked him into it. With the help of his parents," Milos added.

Uncle Goran nodded as if he was beginning to understand. "Can you tell me why this girl's cousin damaged Bojan's truck?"

Bojan gave a warning look, but Milos wasn't going to lie to Uncle Goran, and he felt it was time the truth came out. "Bojan broke the window in her family's store."

"I only did it to get even with them for breaking my arm," Bojan muttered.

"Can you tell me why they broke his arm?" Uncle Goran asked Milos, ignoring Bojan.

"He sprayed a message on the window of their store."

"What did the message say?"

"What his bumper sticker says."

"You sprayed that message of hate on the window of their store?" Uncle Goran said, raising his voice. "Why did you do it?"

Bojan shrugged. "It was after they attacked the World Trade Center."

"The people who own that store didn't attack us."

"Muslims attacked us, and they're Muslims."

"I don't care what they are. They're people like us, trying to make a living. And you know what? They were right to break your arm."

"They weren't right to hurt him," Aunt Vidra objected.

"Well, they were right to stop him from spraying messages on their window."

"I agree with Aunt Vidra," Milos said. "They weren't right to hurt him, and they weren't right to damage his truck. It's never right to get even with people."

They all looked at him speechless.

"My girlfriend's family lost everything they had in Bosnia, and she lost her mother. Our family lost everything we had, and my mother lost her brother. We don't want that to happen again in America. We want our families to make peace."

"We're not at war with this girl's family," Aunt Vidra said.

"Our son is," Uncle Goran said. "And I agree with Milos. We don't want what happened in Bosnia to happen again in America."

"My girlfriend's cousin is willing to pay for the damage to your truck," he told Bojan. "So you should agree not to get even with him."

"That sounds reasonable," Uncle Goran said. "We're repairing the truck at the shop now, and we won't charge for the labor, so it won't cost that much."

"They should pay for the labor," Aunt Vidra said.

"No, they shouldn't. It sounds like our son started this war, so we have some responsibility."

"The guy will pay whatever it costs," Milos said, willing to contribute if necessary.

"They should do more than pay for the damage," Bojan said.

"Why should they?" Uncle Goran asked.

"It's my *truck*," Bojan said.

"He took such good care of it," Aunt Vidra said.

"It's enough that they pay for the damage," Uncle Goran said. "Bojan, tell Milos you'll accept the payment, and tell him you won't do anything more to that family."

Bojan hesitated, looking at his mother as if he hoped she would rescue him.

"Tell him. Now," Uncle Goran said in a voice of absolute authority.

"I'll accept the payment," Bojan said hoarsely, "and I won't do anything more to that family."

"I take that as a promise, and I expect you not to break it."

"Don't worry. I won't."

Milos was awakened by the doorbell. According to the clock on the table next to his bed, it was four-fifteen, and he couldn't imagine who would be visiting at that hour unless there was an emergency downstairs.

He quickly pulled on a pair of jeans and went to the door, barefoot, a few steps ahead of his mother, in her robe.

When he opened the door he saw a tall police officer.

"I'm sorry to bother you so early in the morning," the officer said. "Does Milos Stojanovic live here?"

"Yes. I'm Milos," he said, realizing that something had gone wrong.

"Would you like to come in?" his mother asked.

He stepped out of the way and let the officer enter the living room. By now his father, in his robe, had joined them.

"What is it?" his father asked, bewildered.

"I'm investigating a crime that occurred early this morning," the officer explained. "Someone torched a store on McLean Avenue, and the owner believes it was a member of your family. My partner's talking with him now."

"Torched?" his father said as if he didn't understand the word.

"Someone set fire to the store."

"I hope no one was hurt," his mother said anxiously.

"No, thank God. But a lot of damage was done to the store. It's Joe's Deli," the officer said. "I understand that your son knows the owners."

"I do know them," Milos said. "They're the uncle and aunt of my girlfriend."

"Girlfriend?" his father asked.

"It's all right," his mother told his father. "I knew about it."

"Do you know that your cousin and your girlfriend's cousin are at war with each other?" the officer asked Milos.

"Yes. I'm aware of it."

"Did you hear your cousin say anything about torching the store?"

"No. In fact, he agreed last night to accept a payment from my girlfriend's cousin for the damage to his truck."

"We know about the truck, and it looks like a motive."

"But he promised his father he wouldn't do anything more to that family."

"Did you see him leave the house last night?"

"No. I didn't. He can't use his truck now."

"Someone could have picked him up."

"I didn't see anyone pick him up."

"So as far as you know, he was home all night?"

"As far as I know," Milos said. He knew it wasn't necessary for him to point out to the officer that Bojan could have planned the attack during the day and not left the house all night in order to have an alibi.

"I know it's hard," the officer said, "to give information about someone in your family, but if you can tell me anything to help us in our investigation, I really would appreciate it."

"If we knew anything, we would tell you," his mother said.

"How bad was the damage to the store?" Milos asked.

"The store was totaled. They'll have to start over again."

"They must have insurance."

"I assume they do. But from what I could see, the store was supporting two families, and they won't have any income for a while."

"The poor people," his mother said with sympathy.

"I should also tell you," the officer said, "that there was evidently a fight between the guys were who watching the store and the guys who torched it. And at least one of the guys was wounded."

"Was he wounded badly?" Milos asked.

"We don't know. There was a lot of blood."

"So you didn't see him?"

"They took him away."

"Then I guess you don't know which side he was on."

"It doesn't matter. Whichever side he was on, it could lead to more bloodshed."

"Lord, have mercy," his mother said.

"Well, if you can think of anything," the officer said, handing a card to him, "please contact me. And again, I'm sorry to bother you so early in the morning."

When the police officer had left, his father asked: "What's this about a war between Bojan and your girlfriend's cousin?"

"Why didn't you tell us about it?" his mother asked.

"I didn't want to worry you, and I thought we could stop it."

"How did it start?" his father asked.

"Bojan sprayed a message on the window of their store. It said: 'Muslims go home.' "

"You have a Muslim girlfriend?"

"I knew about it," his mother said. "There's nothing wrong with his having a Muslim girlfriend. Before the war, we all got along."

"Yeah, we did. But is that what started the war between Bojan and her cousin?"

"No," Milos said. "They started fighting before they knew about us. It happened by chance that Bojan sprayed the window of her family's store."

"Is that how Bojan's arm got broken?"

"They did it to get even with him."

"And what did Bojan do to get even with them?"

"He broke their window."

His father nodded. "And to get even, they damaged his truck."

"It sounds familiar," his mother said sadly.

"I don't understand why it happened," Milos said. "Last night Bojan agreed to accept a payment from my girlfriend's cousin for the damage to his truck, and they were going to meet at the college today. So why would he go and torch the store?"

"If he didn't leave the house," his father said, "he didn't go and do anything."

"Well, he has guys who could have done it for him."

"You mean the guys that the officer mentioned?"

"Yeah, they belong to a gang in Yonkers."

"Do the police know this?"

"I think they do."

"Well, in case they don't, you should tell them."

"Okay. The problem is," he added, "Amira's cousin has guys who belong to a gang in the Bronx."

"So Bojan is involved in a gang war," his father said glumly. "He doesn't understand that wars get out of control. And maybe this one got out of control."

Milos considered the implications. "So his guys could have torched the store without his telling them to do it."

"They could have. And the same thing could happen with your girlfriend's cousin. His guys could do something to us without his telling them to do it."

"You should tell the police about them," his mother said. "They might still be downstairs talking with Bojan."

"Okay," Milos said. He went to his room and put on his shoes. In the hall he noticed through the open door of their room that his sisters were sound asleep. And he wished he was still asleep, oblivious of what was happening.

The police were leaving when he got downstairs, but he caught them in their car.

"I thought of something that might help you," he told the officer in the driver's seat through the open window.

"We need all the help we can get," the officer said, indicating that their meeting with Bojan hadn't been helpful.

"I think gangs are involved in this war."

"We know they're involved. Can you give us any details?"

"Yeah. My cousin has guys from a gang in Yonkers, and my girlfriend's cousin has guys from a gang in the Bronx."

"Do you know the names of these gangs?"

"No, but I met two guys from the gang in the Bronx. They followed me and told me to stop seeing Amira."

"What did they look like?"

"They had shaved heads and tattoos."

"They all have shaved heads and tattoos. Did you ever see the guys from Yonkers?"

"No, I never saw them. I only saw the guys from the Bronx."

"Well, if you can find out the names of these gangs," the officer told him, "it would help us stop this stupid war."

"Okay. I'll try," he told the officer.

As soon as they had gone, his cousin appeared.

"I saw you talking with the police," Bojan said. "What did you tell them?"

"Nothing they didn't already know."

"What did you *tell* them?" Bojan repeated, encroaching on his personal space.

"I told them gangs are involved in your war, and they said they already knew that."

Bojan snarled: "Your girlfriend's cousin may have a gang doing things for him, but I don't have one."

"Then who were those guys I saw you with?"

"They're drinking buddies."

"Sure they are."

"I swear to God," Bojan said. "I didn't have anything to do with torching the store. I didn't even know about it until the police told me."

"If you didn't do it, then who did?"

"How should I know?"

"Do you think your guys could have done it on their own?"

"They could have," Bojan said. "But they always only did what I asked them to do."

"Well, maybe you don't control them anymore."

Bojan looked worried by the possibility. If his guys were caught they would tell the police he had ordered them to torch the store even if he hadn't.

Back upstairs, Milos called the only number he had for Amira, the number of the store. But the phone rang as it did when there was a problem in the service. So he had to decide whether he was more likely to find her at the store or at the college.

He decided to try the college first. If she wasn't there for religion class, then he could take a bus to McLean Avenue and hope to find her there.

As he left the house he ran into Pamet, and they headed off for Nepperhan Avenue, where Pamet would catch a bus to the Yonkers train station and from there a train to the city.

"I heard what happened," Pamet said as they walked along Woodland. "I'm so sorry."

"Do you think your brother did it?" Milos asked.

"I know he didn't do it himself. He was home all night."

"Do you think he had other people do it?"

"I don't think so. He really seems upset. I mean, not as much as he was when they damaged his truck, but almost as much."

Milos considered. "So do you believe him when he says he had nothing to do with it?"

"Yeah, I do. I saw his face when the police told him what had happened, and he was surprised."

"Are you sure he wasn't just acting surprised?"

"Bojan isn't a good actor. To be a good actor, you need to have an imagination."

"I assume the police told him that a guy was wounded."

"Yeah, they told him," Pamet said. "They asked him if gangs were involved. He said they weren't, but I think the police suspect they are."

"I think they are. I think it's turned into a gang war."

They were walking down Montague Street toward Nepperhan. "What do you think will happen now?"

"I don't know. I thought we were going to end it tonight, but a guy was wounded, and if he was a member of Bojan's gang then they'll want to get even with the other gang."

"Yeah, they will."

"And they'll blame Bojan."

"So he's in trouble," Pamet said. "The thing is, if he didn't tell them to torch the store, he's not responsible for the guy getting wounded."

"But he's responsible for getting them involved."

"Yeah. Well, if I can do anything to help you end it, let me know."

"I will," Milos said. "And thanks for the information."

They parted at Nepperhan, where they would take buses in different directions.

As he rode to the college Milos prayed that Amira would be there for religion class so he could at least comfort her. By now he was inclined to believe that Bojan hadn't told his gang to torch the store, but he realized that if Bojan and Hasan were no longer in control then he and Amira had less influence. And he wondered if this happened in all wars: they started with something gratuitous, and they escalated out of control.

He was waiting outside the classroom when Amira appeared. Though there were people all around them, she came into his arms and pressed her face against his shoulder, sobbing.

"They destroyed our store," she managed to say.

"I know," he said. "The police told us."

At that moment he saw Sister Maura, who had stopped in the hallway behind Amira. With a look of compassion she said: "I can see there's something you need to talk about, so don't worry about the class. I'll give you an excused absence."

"Thank you, sister," Milos said.

"So can I assume that we won't have the meeting tonight?"

"Yes. We have to think of something else."

"Well, God be with you."

With his arm around Amira he guided her out of Wagner Hall and onto the terrace that overlooked the river. It was another nice, warm sunny day.

"I'm so sorry," Milos said when they were well beyond the people on the terrace.

"It's not your fault."

"I feel it is."

"I understand. I feel the same way when Hasan does something to your family. I mean, I know it's not my fault, but I can't help feeling it is."

They walked in silence for a while, and then Milos said: "You know, when I talked with Bojan last night, he agreed to accept payment for the damage to his truck. And according to his brother,

Bojan was surprised when the police came and told him what happened to your family's store."

"You don't think he did it?"

"I don't think he did. I think his gang did it."

"If they did, they had a fight with Hasan's gang. There were blood stains on the sidewalk in front of the store."

"The police told us a guy was wounded."

"My uncle made Hasan agree not to do anything to get even, but if his gang has their own reason for getting even, then he might not be able to stop them."

"That's what I'm afraid of," Milos said. "Things might have gotten out of control."

They left the terrace and headed toward the athletic fields, but then Amira took his arm and said: "Come on. I want to show you something."

"What?" he asked, curious.

But she said nothing more until they reached a grotto on the walk that led to the convent. It was built of mossy stones and shaded with foliage, with a fountain fed by a stream that flowed down to the river. In the center was a life-sized statue of the Virgin Mary, carved out of white marble, whose inclined face gazed at them with enduring compassion.

"You know who she is?" Milos asked.

"Of course I do. She's the Virgin Mary. She was the mother of Jesus. She's mentioned many times in the Quran, which has a whole chapter about her. I can tell you what the angel said when he told her she would have a baby."

"What did he say?"

"The angel said: 'Mary, God has chosen you and made you pure. He has truly chosen you above all women.' "

"You call her Mary?"

"We call her Maryam."

"Maryam?"

"Yeah." She paused, overcome with emotion. "That was my mother's name."

With his heart going out to her, Milos enfolded her in his arms and comforted her, saying: "I'm so sorry you lost her."

"I didn't lose her. She's in heaven, watching over me."

For a long time he held her in the presence of her mother, who he hoped would bless their relationship. When they finally turned away and continued walking toward the athletic fields, he realized that though they had different religions, they had something vital in common which they shared in their hearts.

They carried the feeling with them to the path, where they paused to look out at the river. Below, a tug was towing a barge downstream, leaving a wake behind it. The leaves on the trees at the top of the Palisades were still green, with just the slightest hint of yellow.

When they had sat down on the bench Amira said: "If Hasan and Bojan can't control their gangs, then we should ask the police to control them."

"I agree," he said. "But we don't know who they are."

"Then we have to find out who they are."

"Our cousins know who they are."

"Well, we have to get our cousins to tell us."

"But if the police go after them," he said, "the gangs will know that someone told them."

"Our cousins can say they didn't tell them."

"Yeah. They can. And the police can say they had other sources of information."

"You think we should try it?"

"I can't think of anything else."

They sat in silence for a while, holding hands and gazing at the peaceful river, and then Amira said: "My uncle thinks it'll take several months to rebuild the store."

"What'll your family do for money?"

"I think my father can get unemployment."

"Will that pay enough for you to live on?"

"No, but it'll help," she said positively.

"Could he get another job until the store reopens?"

"He's a great cook, but he doesn't know much English. He

speaks Bosnian at work, and he speaks Bosnian at home. I try to teach him English, but it's hard for him. I mean, having his daughter teach him."

"Are there any restaurants where they speak Bosnian?"

"My uncle says there's one in Queens. But my father doesn't have a car, so even if he could get a job there I don't know how he'd get there."

"If you want to work at the A&P they have openings there."

"Yeah, that could help," she said. "But first I have to help my father apply for unemployment."

He put his arm around her waist. "You know, more than ever I feel like getting into a boat and floating down the river with you."

"I do too," she said, leaning her head against his shoulder.

"But we can't run away."

"We can't, though I wish we could."

They sat for a while without talking, enjoying this time of peace together. Finally, conscious of their time being limited, he said: "The police officer told me that if I could find out the name of Bojan's gang, it would help them stop the war. So I'll talk with Bojan and find out the name of his gang."

"Okay. I'll talk with Hasan and find out the name of his gang."

"We can give that information to the police, and maybe they can stop this war."

"If they can't," she said, "what do you think Hasan's gang will do next?"

"I've been wondering about that," he said. "If there's any logic in what they do, they'll go after Bojan's truck and destroy it."

"Then he should hide it."

"It's in my uncle's shop, so they won't find it in our driveway."

"Could they find it in your uncle's shop?"

"I guess they could."

"Then he should put his truck somewhere else."

"I'll tell him to do that."

They stayed at the spot until it was time for their next class, and then they headed back toward Wagner Hall, holding hands.

That evening after dinner he asked Bojan to go out into the yard and talk. He had found Bojan watching the news on television with Uncle Goran. The news was about the expected invasion of Afghanistan.

"We'll clobber those guys," Bojan said as they left the house. It sounded as if he was talking about a sports event.

"I hope we don't go to war," Milos said. "A lot of innocent people will be killed."

"They're not innocent. They're Muslims."

"They're human beings like us."

"If you didn't have a Muslim girlfriend, you wouldn't say that."

"Yeah, I would."

"Then you're a traitor," Bojan said, sitting in one of the patio chairs. "The fucking Muslims attacked us, so they're the enemy. And you're on their side."

"I'm not on anyone's side," Milos said, sitting in another chair. "I want peace."

"We won't have peace until we've killed them all."

"That's not my idea of peace."

"Well, it's my idea."

Milos decided it was pointless to argue. "Let's talk about this other war, the one between you and my girlfriend's cousin."

"What about it?"

"If someone doesn't stop them, her cousin's gang will get even with you."

"They have no reason to get even with me. I didn't tell anyone to torch that store."

"They don't know you didn't," Milos pointed out. "They only know your gang did it."

"They're not in a gang. They're drinking buddies."

"Whoever they are, you got them involved in this thing, and the other gang knows that, so they hold you responsible."

"They don't care about the store."

"I know they don't, but they do care about the guy who was wounded protecting it."

"Don't worry," Bojan said. "They won't come after me. They'll go after the guys who did it."

"If they don't know who did it, they'll come after you to find out who did it."

"They know who did it."

"Are you sure?"

"No. I'm not sure."

"Do you want them to come after you?"

"No. But I don't think they will."

"I think they will."

Bojan squirmed uneasily. "So what the hell do you want me to do?"

"I want you to tell me the name of your gang."

"What good will *that* do?"

"I'll tell the police who they are," Milos said, "and the police can watch for the other gang to go after them."

"That won't stop them from coming after me."

"I'll get the police to protect you."

"Why would they protect me?"

"Because they need you as a witness."

Bojan frowned. "If my guys found out I told the police who they are—"

"You're not going to tell the police. I am."

"They'll still think I did."

"The police will tell them it wasn't you."

"They won't believe them."

"Then don't tell me the name of your gang," Milos said in frustration. "Just sit here on your butt and wait for the other gang to come after you."

Bojan was silent, and then he said: "All right. I'll tell you—on one condition. Your girlfriend has to find out the name of her cousin's gang."

"She's going to find out this evening."

"But she hasn't yet."

"I think she will. Her cousin's father is putting a lot of pressure on him."

Bojan looked at him closely. "You haven't talked with my father about this, have you?"

"I haven't talked with him since last night."

"Well, don't talk with him about it."

"I won't. I promise. So when are you going to tell me the name of your gang?"

"When your girlfriend tells you the name of her cousin's gang."

"I'll try to reach her tonight," Milos said, figuring he could get her home phone number from information. "I'll let you know as soon as I know."

"Okay," Bojan said, no longer sounding belligerent.

Before leaving him, Milos advised him to get his truck out of the shop and hide it somewhere, but Bojan didn't seem concerned, evidently relying on his gang for protection.

Back in his family's apartment Milos went into the kitchen, where they kept the phone, and he called information. There were two people listed in Yonkers with Amira's last name: A. Hasanic and T. Hasanic. He remembered that her father's name was Tarik from when her aunt had introduced him, so he asked the operator for the number of T. Hasanic.

He called the number, and Amira answered.

"Hi. It's Milos," he said, relieved to hear her voice.

"Hi," she said, sounding glad that he had called.

"I just talked with Bojan, and he agreed to tell me the name of his gang."

"That's great. I haven't been able to talk with Hasan. He hasn't come home yet. I asked my aunt to let me know as soon as he comes home."

"So we can go to the police tomorrow."

"Is there a police station near the college?"

"Yeah, there is. It's on Shonnard Place," he said, having gone there with his father. "It's not far from North Broadway. So you could take the bus to Shonnard and walk there."

"What time should we meet there?"

"I think we should get there by eight in the morning."

"Okay. I'll see you then."

"I love you."

"I love you too."

After hanging up he could hear only her last four words, which resonated in his mind like an assurance that everything would be all right.

He studied for a while, reviewing his notes from biology, and then he went to bed. Though he hadn't heard back from Amira, he expected to hear from her in the morning so he could tell Bojan she had found out the name of her cousin's gang. And he went to sleep believing that the next day they could go to the police with information about the gangs.

He was awakened by the doorbell at about the same time as the previous day, and for a moment he thought he was only having a nightmare. But he realized that he was awake, and after pulling on his jeans he hurried to the door.

When he opened it he saw the same tall police officer.

"I'm sorry to bother you again so early," the officer said, "but there's been another incident."

"What happened?" he asked, stepping aside to let the officer come in.

"They bombed your uncle's shop."

"Oh, my God." He felt sick.

"They put the explosive in your cousin's truck, so it looks like they were getting even with him for torching the store."

"But he didn't torch the store."

"I know," the officer said. "That's why I said it looks like they were getting even with him. I think they were really getting even with the other gang."

"Then why did they go after the shop?"

"The other gang was there, protecting it. Or, more likely, protecting his truck."

Milos could see how Bojan's love for his truck had drawn the other gang to the shop, and he could guess what else had happened. "Was anyone wounded?"

"It looks that way. There were blood stains on the pavement in front of the shop."

By then his mother and father had joined them.

"*Šta se desilo?*" his father asked.

"They bombed Uncle Goran's shop."

"Oh, no," his mother said, bringing her hand up to her mouth.

"There was a lot of damage," the officer said.

"Who did it?" his mother asked.

"We think a gang did it. But we don't know which one."

"My girlfriend and I were trying to find out the names of the gangs so we could give you that information. We were planning to give it to you this morning."

"It's not too late," the officer said. "At least they haven't killed anyone yet. Can you give me the information now?"

"I don't have it. My cousin was going to tell me the name of his gang as soon as my girlfriend found out the name of her cousin's gang."

"And that never happened?"

"I expected to hear from her this morning."

"Well, if you hear from her, let me know. My partner's working on your cousin now, but if we can't get the information from him, maybe you can."

"Okay. I'll let you know."

When the police officer had gone downstairs Milos said to his parents: "So now our family's in the same situation as Amira's family."

"I never imagined that such a thing could happen here in America," his mother said.

"It can happen anywhere," his father said despondently.

"It started with an act of hate," Milos said.

"That's how it started in Bosnia," his mother said.

"It's how America's next war started," his father said.

"But an act of hate doesn't have to start a war," Milos said. "If we responded by loving our enemies and praying for those who hate us, there wouldn't be wars."

"In another world," his father said.

"I still believe it's possible in this world," his mother said.

"I do too," Milos said. "And I still believe we can stop this war from going any further."

"At least they haven't killed anyone yet," his mother said.

"So how are you going to stop it?" his father asked.

"By helping the police, by bringing the two gangs together. Whatever it takes. But we're going to find a way to stop it."

"Just be careful," his mother said.

"We don't want anything to happen to you," his father said.

"Don't worry," Milos said, believing his love would protect him.

Chapter 11

AMIRA DIDN'T SLEEP well that night. She kept waking up and alertly listening for the sound of Hasan coming home, and even though after midnight it was too late for her to go upstairs and see him, she couldn't rest on the assumption that she could talk with him early in the morning because she worried about the possibility that something had happened to him. For the first time in her life she needed Hasan—to stop the war between him and Milos's cousin.

She finally dozed off and awoke at six, the usual hour. She dressed and went to the kitchen, where she found her father sitting at the table with a cup of coffee and a roll.

"*Dobro jutro,*" her father said. "Did you sleep well?"

"Yes," she lied. She leaned over and gently kissed the back of his neck. "I have to go and talk with Hassan. I'll be right back."

"On your way, try to wake up your brother."

She stopped in her brother's room and gave him a nudge. "Kashir, wake up."

He groaned and rolled away from her.

"It's quarter after six. You can't miss the bus."

"I'm awake," he complained as if he was being punished.

She left him and went upstairs and rang the bell, hoping that Hasan would come to the door.

Instead, it was Aunt Malika, who said: "Good morning."

"Good morning," she said. "Is Hasan up?"

"I think he's still sleeping. He was out until almost three in the morning."

"He has to go to work, doesn't he?"

"Oh, yes. So he can't sleep past seven."

"When he gets up, could you ask him to come down and see me?"

"Of course. I know you'll support what his father told him."

"I will," she said. "Milos and I are trying to make peace."

"God bless you, child," Aunt Malika said. "Your mother in heaven is proud of you."

When she returned to her family's apartment her father told her that Milos had called. He had left a phone number, which she called right away. A girl, who she figured was one of Milos's sisters, answered the phone.

Amira asked for Milos and waited anxiously.

"Hi," he said, sounding weary.

"Did something happen?"

"They bombed my uncle's shop."

"Oh, no. I'm sorry."

"There was a lot of damage. The thing is, they put the bomb in Bojan's truck, so obviously it was aimed at him."

"Was anyone hurt?"

"Yeah, a guy was wounded," Milos said. "Bojan had his gang watching the shop, protecting his truck, and there must have been a fight between the gangs."

"I'm still waiting to talk with Hasan. I didn't have a chance last night. He was out until three in the morning."

"Do you think he was involved in the bombing?"

"I don't know. I hope he wasn't."

"Well, we don't have any information for the police," Milos said, "so let's meet at the college. We may have to find another approach."

"I could get there early."

"I could too."

They arranged to meet around nine at their spot at the end of the path.

As she was hanging up the phone she heard a tap on the front door. She went and opened it and saw Hasan looking as if he hadn't gotten any sleep.

"My mom said you wanted to see me."

"Yeah," she said. Deciding it would be better to talk outside where her father couldn't hear them, she went out and closed the door behind her.

"God, I have a headache."

"Where were you last night?"

"I was out," he said, implicitly telling her she didn't need to know where.

"Milos called me a few minutes ago. He told me they bombed his uncle's shop. I hope you weren't involved in it."

"I wasn't," he said, looking upset. "I swear to God."

"I believe you," she said. "But your gang must have done it."

"Well, I didn't ask them to do it. In fact, I haven't seen them since my father threatened to tell the police if I got even with your boyfriend's cousin."

"Milos said a guy was wounded."

"Oh, shit. Was it a guy from his cousin's gang?"

"I don't know, but it doesn't matter which gang he belonged to."

Hasan considered. "I guess it doesn't. If it was a guy from his cousin's gang, they'll want to get even with my gang, and if it was a guy from my gang, they'll want to get even with his cousin's gang. So either way they'll want to get even."

"That's why we have to stop it."

"But how can we stop it?"

"By telling the police the names of the gangs."

Hasan shook his head. "I can't do that. If they ever found out, they'd kill me."

At that moment a police car pulled up in front of the house. As they got out of the car she recognized the tall officer and the hefty officer.

"I'm glad we found you both at home," the tall officer said, coming up the sidewalk. The hefty officer followed him.

"We heard what happened," Amira said.

"How did you hear?"

"My boyfriend called me."

The tall officer stopped in front of Hasan. "Can you tell us where you were between six last night and three this morning?"

"That's easy," Hasan said calmly. "I was in a bar the whole time. I went there after work and I left when they closed."

"What's the name and address of this bar?"

"It's Tony's Garage. It's in the Bronx, on 149th Street near Third Avenue."

"I know the place," the hefty officer said.

"Can you give us the names of people who will verify that you were there?" the tall officer asked Hasan.

"Tony will verify that I was there. And so will Mike."

"Tony's the owner," the hefty officer said. "And Mike's a bartender."

"We'll check with them," the tall officer said. "But that won't get you off the hook. We think your gang planted the bomb."

"I didn't have anything to do with it."

"You didn't tell them to get even with the other gang for torching the store?"

"No. I didn't. I didn't tell them to do anything."

"But you got them involved in your war."

"Yeah. But her boyfriend's cousin started it."

"I don't care who started it. I want to know the name of your gang and where they hang out."

Hasan hesitated. "If they find out I told you, they'll kill me."

"They haven't killed anyone yet," he hefty officer said, "and if they know we're watching them, they're not likely to kill you. They don't want to face a murder charge."

"Well, I need time to think about it."

"We don't have time," the tall officer said. "If you don't give us that information right now, we'll take you in for questioning. And when they hear you're in custody, they'll assume the worst."

"Okay, okay." Hasan gave them the information.

"Thanks for your cooperation. We'll have more questions, so don't go too far way. You understand?"

"I understand. And please don't tell my parents I was in a bar."

The tall officer cocked his head. "Why do you care?"

"Drinking alcohol is against our religion."

"Then don't do it. And don't get involved with gangs. What those guys do is against your religion."

When the police had left, Hasan said: "I hope you're happy."

"I won't be happy until we make peace," Amira said. "But thanks for giving that information to the police. It's a step in the right direction."

Hasan looked doubtful.

Back in the house, she found her father at the kitchen table with yesterday's newspaper in front of him. They sold the *Daily News* and the *New York Post* at the store, and if there were any unsold papers at the end of the day, he brought one home. It was a way of learning English.

"What was that about?" he asked, looking up from the paper.

She told him what had happened.

"Bog nam pomogne. What will Milos's family do?"

"The same thing we're doing. They'll rebuild their business, and in the meantime they'll get unemployment."

"I wish I could find a job in the meantime."

"We'll try to find one."

"Are we still going to the unemployment office today?"

"Yes. We can go this afternoon." She had to go there with him because he wouldn't be able to fill out the forms and answer the questions without her help.

After a silence her father said: "Remember the birthday party we gave you at our restaurant? You were nine years old."

"It's one of my happiest memories," she said, putting her hand on his shoulder.

"It's one of mine too. But the happiest memory is when you were born."

"You weren't unhappy that I was a girl?"

"Oh, no. I wanted a girl. And I thanked God that you were a girl."

"Then two years later God rewarded you with a boy."

"You're my gifts from God, the two of you. And I'm glad we came to America. You'll both have better lives here."

"I believe we will. We just have to stop this war between Hasan and Milos's cousin."

"Well, don't get too involved in that," her father said, laying his hand on top of her hand. "I don't want anything to happen to you."

"Don't worry. I'll be careful."

She let Rafid know she was going to the college earlier, and she walked to the bus stop, wearing a jacket for the first time this season. It was cooler in the mornings now, but if the sun came out it warmed up enough by the afternoon so she didn't need the jacket, and then she stuffed it into her backpack with her books and notepads.

On the bus there were several women wearing scrubs of different colors, evidently going to work at St. John's Hospital. Two of them, who sat in front of her, were talking in Spanish. She caught a few words, but she couldn't follow their conversation, and she understood what not speaking English was like for her father. She asked God to help him get a job while Uncle Ahmed was rebuilding the store.

When she got off at the college, instead of going into Wagner Hall she walked around it and across the athletic field to the path that overlooked the river. She found Milos waiting for her, sitting on the bench.

He got up, and she hugged him, saying: "I'm sorry."

"It's all right. We've survived worse things."

"I guess we have."

As they went to sit down on the grass he said: "We should have a blanket. And when it gets colder we'll have to find another spot."

"Yeah, somewhere inside."

He was silent for a while, and then he said: "The police came to our house this morning. I told them we were trying to find out which gangs are involved in the war between our cousins."

"They came to our house too, and they got Hasan to give them information about his gang."

"That's good. But they couldn't get Bojan to tell them. I talked with him after the police left, and he has another idea."

"What's his idea?"

"He wants the gangs to have a meeting and make peace."

"Why would they do that?" she asked.

"The police said there were blood stains on the pavement in front of the shop. So at least two guys have been wounded so far, and if they keep fighting, sooner or later someone will get killed."

"Well, based on what the police told us, the gangs don't want to face a murder charge."

"I'm sure they don't want to face any charge. And if our cousins don't testify against them, they might not be charged with torching the store or bombing the shop. So if they stop fighting now, they might get away with what they've done."

"Is your cousin going to contact his gang?"

"He said he was going to talk with them today."

"Then Hasan should contact his gang. I'll talk with him this evening."

"Okay. If our cousins want to stop the war, they have to get the gangs to stop it. And maybe now the gangs want to stop it."

"I hope they do."

He checked his watch. "It's almost ten. We better go to class. Our other professors won't be as understanding as Sister Maura."

"You're right. We don't want to lose our scholarships."

He got up and gave her his hand to help her up.

They paused to look at the view of the river and the blurred skyline of the city. Three weeks had passed since the attack, and rescue workers were still laboring in the rubble, no longer in the hope of finding survivors but of finding remains.

That evening she talked with Hasan after dinner. They sat on the front steps of the house while some children played in the street.

"Milos's cousin wants the gangs to have a meeting and make peace," she told Hasan.

"What if they don't want peace?" Hasan asked her.

"Well, maybe they've had enough of this war. At least two of their guys have been wounded."

"How do you figure?"

"One at the store, and the other at the shop. And if one guy from each gang was wounded, then they're even now."

"Yeah, they would be," Hasan said.

"Milos's cousin said he was going to contact his gang and try to get them to meet somewhere."

"And you want me to contact my gang?"

"Yeah, I do. I'm asking you."

Hasan looked at her as if he was imagining how she could repay him, and then he said: "All right. But if they agree to have a meeting, I need to know where."

"I'll find out. So you're going to contact them?"

"Yeah. I'll talk with them tonight."

She was so happy that she leaned over and kissed Hasan on the cheek. As she turned to go she noticed that he was holding the tips of his fingers to the spot with a look of wonder at the kind of love she had shown him. It gave her hope that he would stop lusting for her.

With her and Milos intermediating between their cousins, it was agreed that the gangs would have a meeting at nine o'clock on Saturday night in Tibbetts Park.

In her prayers on Friday she thanked God for the meeting.

She and Milos had arranged to meet on Saturday afternoon, so she took a bus to the college and walked to their secluded spot. He had brought a blanket, which they spread on the grass and sat down on, facing the river.

"Will you be allowed to go out tonight?" Milos asked.

"I'm not going to ask my aunt," she said. "I'm going to ask my father. I'll tell him we're going out on a date."

"What if he won't let you?"

"I'm sure he will. But he'll make me promise to be home by eleven."

"That should give us enough time."

"How will we get there?"

"I'm going to borrow my father's car."

"You have a driver's license?"

"Oh, yeah. My father wanted me to get one just in case."

"My aunt doesn't want me to get a driver's license. She doesn't have one."

"Well, luckily we can get around by bus. The way things are now, I can't imagine having the money to buy a car."

They lay down on the blanket, enjoying the warmth of the sun and the proximity of their bodies. It wasn't long before they were kissing.

She loved kissing Milos and being kissed by him. She could feel love flowing both ways and unifying them in a state of bliss. And she was aware of her mother in heaven smiling down at her, pleased that she had found such happiness on earth.

Later, as she was lying on her back and gazing up at the blue sky, she said: "I have an idea. I think we should go and find Sister Maura and tell her what's happening."

"I had the same idea," Milos said. "I must have read your mind."

"Or else I read your mind."

"If we read each other's mind, then where did we get the idea?"

"Maybe we got it from up there."

"Maybe we did."

They rolled toward each other and gazed into each other's eyes. She felt his heart coming out to her, and her heart going out to him.

"I love you," he said, touching her face.

"I love you too," she said, kissing his fingers.

When they got up he folded the blanket and stuffed it into his backpack.

Holding hands, they walked to the building where Sister Maura had her office. There was no one in the hall, but her door was open, and they found her at her desk.

"Come in," she said, welcoming them. "I need a break."

At her invitation they sat down in the two chairs in front of her desk, which had piles of papers on top of it.

"So what's the latest?" Sister Maura asked.

"The bad news is," Milos began, "our cousins brought gangs into their war."

"Gangs?" Sister Maura looked concerned. "From where?"

"My cousin brought in a gang from Yonkers."

"My cousin brought in a gang from the Bronx."

"Do your cousins belong to gangs?"

"No. But they know some members," Milos said.

"And what have the gangs done for them?" Sister Maura asked.

"My cousin's gang torched her family's store, and her cousin's gang bombed our family's auto shop."

"Lord, have mercy. How are your families?"

"They'll survive," Amira said. "They've been through worse things."

Sister Maura nodded as if she could imagine. "So what's the good news?"

"The good news is," Milos said, "our cousins have arranged a meeting between the gangs so they can make peace."

"The meeting is tonight," Amira said, "in Tibbetts Park."

"Are you going to be there?" Sister Maura asked.

"Oh, yes. We can help them make peace."

"With our love," Milos said.

"You expect your cousins to start loving each other?"

"No," Amira said. "But do we expect them to stop hating each other."

"That would be a start," Sister Maura said. "But what about the gangs? Do they want peace?"

"If our cousins hadn't brought them into their war," Milos said, "they wouldn't be fighting."

"But they're fighting now. Why would they stop?"

"Some guys from the gangs have been wounded, and if they keep fighting, someone might get killed. And then the police would charge them with murder."

"So you think the gangs have had enough?"

"Yeah, that's what we think."

"Well, the fact that they've agreed to have a meeting supports what you think. And if they don't have anything at stake, they have no reason to keep fighting."

"They do have a reason—the guys who were wounded," Milos pointed out. "But if one guy from each gang was wounded, then they're even now."

"If they think they're even," Sister Maura said, "they may stop fighting. The problem is, there are people who never think they're even."

"Like our cousins," Amira said.

"For them it's personal," Milos said.

"What is it for the gangs?" Sister Maura asked.

"I guess it's business."

"They're doing it for money?"

"Yeah. Why else would they have gotten involved? The guys from Yonkers aren't Serbs, and the guys from the Bronx aren't Bosniaks."

"What are they?" Sister Maura asked.

"I don't know. I assume they're Americans. So what reason do they have to hate each other?"

"What reason do your cousins have to hate each other?"

"They don't have a reason," Amira said. "They were here in America when the war started in Bosnia. So they're using other people's hate."

"Other people's hate," Sister Maura said. "I like that expression. It gets right to the heart of the matter. And we have a lot of that in America."

"If our cousins are using other people's hate," Milos said, "then maybe they can use other people's love."

"He means our love for each other," Amira said.

"I know what he means," Sister Maura said, smiling. "God bless both of you. But be careful tonight. I don't want anything to happen to you."

"Don't worry," Milos said. "We have our love to protect us."

Amira was waiting outside the house when Milos arrived in his father's car. She went around quickly and got into the car, not wanting to give her aunt time to look out the window and spot her. Sitting in the front seat next to Milos, she felt as if they really were going out on a date, and for a moment she forgot their mission.

"Are you all right?" Milos asked.

"Yeah. Are you?"

"Yeah. I told my parents I was going to a movie with you, and they believed me. I feel bad about lying to them, but I couldn't tell them the truth."

"I know. I told my father we were going out on a date."

"Well, if everything goes well, maybe we'll have some time together."

"That would be nice." She said a silent prayer.

Milos drove carefully. Though she didn't drive, she could tell that he was compensating for his lack of experience, and she was at ease.

The plan was to leave their cars on a street near the park and to walk from there to the place where they were supposed to meet. When they got there they didn't see anyone else around, so they waited in the car.

About five minutes later a black car arrived and parked behind them. Bojan, along with three other guys, got out and stood on the sidewalk. Then another black car arrived and parked ahead of them. Hasan, along with three other guys, got out and stood on the sidewalk. Only about twenty feet separated the two groups, but they didn't acknowledge each other.

"We better get out," Milos said.

They got out and stood on the sidewalk between the two groups, who stared at them as if they didn't belong there. A guy with a red headband who was standing next to Bojan sauntered over to them purposefully and asked: "Who are you?"

"I'm Bojan's cousin," Milos said.

"I'm Hasan's cousin," Amira said.

"What are you doing here?"

"We're here to make peace."

"We are too," the guy said. "You can hang around, but stay out of it."

They waited until several more cars arrived, and then they headed into the park, led by the guy with a headband. By now there were about thirty guys, not including Bojan, Hasan, and Milos. They walked in segregated groups, which made it easy to tell that there was about the same number from each gang.

When they reached an open lawn the guy with a headband

stopped and gathered his gang around him. A guy with a beard did the same with the other gang. They talked for a while, and then the two leaders left their groups and parleyed together, far enough removed so that no one could hear what they were saying.

Finally, the two leaders summoned their gangs to draw near.

"We decided not to fight each other," the guy with a headband said. "We got no reason to fight each other."

"This isn't our war," the guy with a beard said. "It's *their* war."

It was clear that he meant Bojan and Hasan.

"So we decided they should fight it out between them," the guy with a headband said.

"What if we don't want to?" Hasan asked.

"You have no choice. You got us involved in your war, and a guy was hurt from each of our gangs. So you should pay for it."

"I paid you money," Bojan said.

"I did too," Hasan said.

"Money's not enough," the guy with a beard said. "We want blood."

"Well, you can't make us fight each other," Bojan said.

"Yeah, we can. If you don't fight, we'll kill you."

"This is for you," the guy with a headband said to Bojan, handing him a knife.

"And this is for you," the guy with a beard said to Hasan, handing him a similar knife.

"We don't want you to kill each other. But we want you to keep fighting until both of you draw blood. You understand?"

Bojan nodded, holding the knife awkwardly in his left hand and looking around for a way to escape. But the gang on his side blocked all ways except to Hasan. And two guys pushed him toward Hasan.

The gang on Hasan's side were doing the same thing, pushing him toward Bojan.

"Stop it!" Milos said, stepping forward.

"Stop pushing them," Amira said, stepping forward too.

"I told you to stay out of it," the guy with a headband told them.

"It's time to stop this stupid war," Milos said.

"It's time to make peace," Amira said.

"Get out of the way," the guy with a beard said.

"You might get hurt," the guy with a headband said.

The guys behind Bojan and Hasan resumed pushing them toward each other.

Milos moved to hold Bojan back, and Amira did the same thing with Hasan. For a while they were the only force that kept Bojan and Hasan apart. And then the guy with a beard, coming from behind her, broke Amira's grip on her cousin and pushed Hasan forward with all his might. The knife he was holding went into Bojan's neck.

"I'm sorry," Hasan cried. "I didn't mean to do that."

With blood gushing from his neck, Bojan fell forward and dropped his knife. Milos, who had been holding him back, picked up the knife in order to take it out of play. But at that moment the guy with a headband grabbed his hand that held the knife and pushed it into Hasan, who was stumbling toward him. The knife went deeply into the soft spot under Hasan's ribs and upward. Hasan plunged forward with blood gushing from his mouth.

"Oh, God," Milos cried, kneeling down beside him.

At that moment Amira joined him, already praying: "In the name of God, the Lord of Mercy, please don't let them die."

"This is bad shit," the guy with a headband said.

"Yeah," the guy with a beard said. "We gotta get out of here."

"Peace, brother."

"Peace."

As the guys from the gangs fled the scene Amira went to Bojan and knelt beside him. From the war in Bosnia she knew what people looked like when they were dead, so she could tell that Bojan was dead.

"Oh, God," she prayed, "have mercy on him, and pardon him, and wash him with water and snow, and cleanse him of his faults, and give him peace."

She went to Milos, who was kneeling by Hasan.

"He's dead," Milos said, with tears in his eyes. "I killed him."

"You didn't kill him. The guy who pushed the knife into him killed him. I saw it happen, and I'll testify before the law, before God."

"I'm so sorry," he said, throwing his arms around her knees and pressing his face to her belly. "I've ruined our lives."

"You haven't ruined anything," she said, stroking his hair. "I still love you."

After a while he looked up at her and asked: "What should we do now?"

"I think we should get out of here. We need time to think."

"About what? I'm guilty of murder."

"No, you're not. You're no more guilty of murder than I am. We were trying to stop them from hurting each other."

"But if we hadn't gotten involved—"

"The same thing would have happened."

"You think it would have?"

"I know it would have."

She gave him her hand and helped him to his feet.

As they walked out of the park with their arms around each other's waists she felt as if they were being expelled from paradise, but she knew she could face the real world. With her mother in heaven watching over her and with Milos by her side, she could face anything.

Chapter 12

THEY COULDN'T GO home now, and since they had nowhere else to go they decided to go to the college, where they could stop and think. But they hadn't gone far when they agreed that they should contact the police and let them know what had happened in the park. They couldn't just leave the bodies of their cousins there.

Milos stopped at the A&P and went inside to the public phone and dialed 911. He knew they could trace the call to the store and eventually to him, but by then he would have turned himself in, so it wasn't a problem.

"I'm calling to report an accident in Tibbetts Park," he told the operator.

"Who's calling? I need to have your name and address and a contact number."

"Just have someone go to Tibbetts Park. Two people were killed there in a fight."

"I need to know exactly where it happened."

He gave the operator directions, and then he hung up.

He went out and got back into the car and pulled out of the parking lot and headed south on Nepperhan to Roberts Avenue and up the steep hill and down to North Broadway, where he turned right and headed north.

Amira was silent, evidently thinking, and since his mind was a jumble of thoughts, Milos kept them to himself and focused on the road in front of them.

When they got to the campus they were stopped at the gate by the security guard, who asked to see his student ID and let them pass. There were no cars coming out of the campus because the evening classes had ended at nine.

Since they both had to pee he parked the car near Wagner Hall, and they walked to the entrance, which was still open, presumably because the classrooms were being cleaned now. They headed toward their respective bathrooms, agreeing to meet outside the women's room. While washing his hands Milos looked at himself in the mirror over the sink, and he was overcome by despair in confronting the face of a killer.

Closing his eyes, he said a prayer he had learned from his mother: "Almighty God, the Father of mercies and God of all comfort, come to my help and deliver me from this difficulty. Take away my fear, anxiety, and distress. Help me to face and endure my difficulty with faith, courage, and wisdom. Grant that this trial may bring me closer to you, for you are my rock and refuge, my comfort and hope, my delight and joy. I trust in your love and compassion. Blessed is your name, Father, Son and Holy Spirit, now and forever. Amen."

He stood outside the women's room and waited for Amira to come out. When she finally did, her face was serene.

"I was praying," she said.

"You were? So was I."

"Did it help?"

"I think so."

After a long silence she said: "We should call our parents and let them know we're all right."

"Yeah, we should, though they have no reason to be worried about us. They don't know where we were tonight."

"But they'll find out when our uncles hear from the police."

"There's a payphone near the cafeteria."

As they walked to the phone Amira said: "I don't want to go home tonight. I want to be with you."

"I want to be with you. But where?"

"We could go to our usual place."

"We could. But you might be cold there."

"Did you bring the blanket?"

"It's in my backpack."

"Well, that would keep us warm enough until we decide what to do next."

"Okay," he said. "So what will you tell your father?"
"I'll tell him I'm going to spend the night with a friend."
"I'll tell my mother the same thing."

They went down the stairs to the hall outside the cafeteria, where the payphone was. He found a quarter in his pocket and gave it to her, letting her go first. Her father was waiting up for her, and he was relieved to hear from her. After several questions he evidently believed her story about spending the night with a friend.

His mother was waiting up for him. As he told her where he was spending the night he reminded himself that technically he wasn't lying, and accepting his story, she gave him her blessing.

With that done they left the building and went to the car, and he got his backpack out of the trunk. He took out the blanket and draped it over her shoulders. And then, holding hands, they walked to the path that overlooked the river.

When they came to the bench they sat on it and gazed across the dark water. On the other side were a few blinking lights, and above them were a million unblinking stars. Below them a tug, with lights on its mast, was pushing a barge against the current.

"Tomorrow morning," Milos said, "I have to go to the police and tell them what I did."

"You didn't do anything," Amira protested. "You picked up that knife to stop anyone else from using it, and that gang leader grabbed your hand and pushed the knife into Hasan."

"I know, but I was holding the knife."

"If you hadn't picked it up, someone else would have used it to kill Hasan. So you shouldn't feel it was your fault."

"I still feel it was my fault."

"But it wasn't your fault that our cousins got into a war with each other."

"Yeah, it was. If I hadn't fallen in love with you, it wouldn't have happened."

"Then it was my fault too."

"Why was it your fault?"

"Because I fell in love with you."

Not wanting her to feel it was her fault, he began to resist his own feeling of responsibility. "They were at war before they knew about us, and they used our relationship as a pretext for escalating. So maybe what happened wasn't our fault."

"Well, it wasn't our fault that we fell in love."

"It wasn't," he agreed. "And we tried to make peace."

She was silent for a while, and then she said: "We know you're innocent, but the police don't know. They'll find your fingerprints on the knife, so they'll think you're guilty. They could charge you with murder and send you to prison."

"They could," he said unhappily.

"I'll testify that you only tried to stop them from fighting, and I'll find other witnesses, and I'll pray that they believe us. But whatever happens, I want us to be married."

"Married? You mean before we go to the police?"

"Yeah. If we wait, they could stop us."

He searched her eyes. "You really want to marry me?"

"Yeah. If we're married," she said, "our families won't be able to separate us."

The more he thought about it, the more he liked the idea of their being married. "And it could help our families make peace."

"So how can we get married?"

"I don't know. We could go to the Virgin Mary and exchange vows in front of her."

"That would be nice, but it wouldn't be a legal marriage."

"Well, I don't know how we could get married legally before we go to the police."

She paused to think. "Could Sister Maura marry us?"

"If she was a priest she could, but I don't know if nuns can marry people. And we can't ask her now. It's almost midnight."

"So we'll ask her in the morning."

"Okay," he said, putting his arm around her.

It was comfortable sitting on the bench, but they couldn't sleep on it, so they decided to go to their secluded place, where they would have the soft grass as a mattress. The blanket was big enough to cover both of them. And snuggled together, they finally went to sleep.

The next morning they were awakened by a pair of birds chirping at each other as if they were having a domestic argument. Milos checked his watch and saw it was a little after six, so he unwrapped the blanket and got up. As soon as he was steady on his feet he gave his hand to Amira and helped her get up.

After folding the blanket they headed back to the athletic fields, strode across them, and climbed the hill to the terrace outside the cafeteria. The door was open, they entered the building, and they walked to the bathrooms, where they freshened up.

Then they went up the stairs and left the building by its main entrance and walked to the convent, pausing on the way to ask the Virgin Mary to help them.

At the visitors' entrance to the convent they were stopped by an old woman behind a desk who looked at them suspiciously.

"We'd like to see Sister Maura," Milos told her.

"Are you students?" the woman asked them.

"Yeah, we're both students."

"What are your names?"

"Milos and Amira."

"Does she know you?"

"Yeah. We're in her religion class."

"Well, it's rather early. Why don't you come back later?"

"We can't come back later."

"Why can't you?"

"Because we need to see her about an urgent matter," Milos said with feeling.

The woman examined him closely as if she was trying to guess what it was. But she finally said: "All right. I'll call her."

They waited for what seemed like a long time until they spotted Sister Maura coming into the hallway, with eyes that were wide awake.

"I'm sorry," the woman behind the desk told her. "These students were very insistent."

"It's all right," Sister Maura said. She looked at Amira and then at Milos as if she had an inkling of why they needed to see her. She asked them to go with her, and she led them into a courtyard that had walls on three sides and the fourth side open, facing the river. She stopped at a bench and indicated that they should sit there, with her in the middle.

She listened while they told her what had happened last night, taking turns. She looked very sad when she heard how Bojan and Hasan had been killed in Tibbetts Park. And she held their hands to console them.

"Milos feels it was his fault," Amira said, "because he fell in love with me. But if it's his fault for falling in love with me, then it's also my fault for falling in love with him."

"It's neither of your faults," Sister Maura said. "You can't be blamed for falling in love. What you feel for each other is a reflection of God's love."

"I know he's innocent, but he might have to go to prison for a while, so we want to be married before that happens. If we're married, our families won't be able to separate us."

"And if we're married," Milos added, "that could help our families make peace."

"So we were wondering if you could marry us."

Sister Maura smiled, shaking her head. "If I were a priest, I could. But I'm only a nun, and our church doesn't give nuns the authority to perform sacraments."

"That's not fair," Milos said.

"It's not fair, but that's how it is. And even if I had the authority, you'd have to get a license from New York State before I could marry you legally."

"We can't be married without a license?" Amira said.

"You can't be married legally."

"Oh. Well, if you can't marry us legally, can you marry us spiritually?"

"How do you mean?"

"By blessing our exchange of vows."

"I'd be happy to do that," Sister Maura said. "Where would you like to exchange vows?"

"In front of the Virgin Mary," Milos said.

"Is that where you would like to exchange vows?" Sister Maura asked Amira.

"Oh, yes. My mother's name is Maryam, our name for Mary. She's in heaven, watching over me. And it'll make her happy to see us exchange vows."

"Then let's go there."

They followed Sister Maura to the grotto, where she prayed: "Blessed Mother, I've brought you two young people who want to exchange marriage vows. I know I don't have the authority to marry them, and they don't have a license, but I trust that you will overlook what they're missing and will bless what they bring to this ceremony."

Milos and Amira stood here, holding hands.

Sister Maura turned from the statue and said: "Milos and Amira, today you celebrate one of life's greatest moments and give recognition to the value of love, as you join together in the vows of marriage. Milos, do you take Amira to be your wife?"

"I do," he said.

"Do you promise to love, honor, cherish, and protect her, forsaking all others and holding only onto her?"

"I do."

"Amira, do you take Milos to be your husband?"

"I do," she said.

"Do you promise to love, honor, cherish, and protect him, forsaking all others and holding only onto him?"

"I do."

"Milos and Amira, as two different threads woven in opposite directions can form a beautiful tapestry, so can your two lives merge together to form a beautiful marriage. To make your marriage work will take love. Remember that love is the core of your marriage, love is the reason you are here. But it will also take trust to know in your hearts you want the best for each other. It will take dedication to stay open to one another, to learn and grow together even when this is not always easy to do. It will take faith to be willing to go forward to tomorrow, never really knowing what tomorrow will bring. It will take commitment to hold true to the journey you both pledge to share together. Milos and Amira, since the two of you have agreed to be joined together in matrimony and have promised your love for each other by these vows, I now declare you husband and wife. Congratulations, you may kiss each other."

Their heads came together in a tender kiss.

"Thank you, sister," they said at almost the same time.

"So where are you going from here?"

"We're going to the police station on Shonnard Place," Milos said. "We're going to tell them what happened last night."

"God be with you," Sister Maura said.

They walked together slowly to the car. As he got into it Milos could tell that Amira shared his feeling of wanting to drive away somewhere and leave the world of hate behind him. But he knew he couldn't run away from it. He had to face it and take the consequences.

He drove out of the campus onto Broadway, turning right and heading toward Shonnard Place.

As they were going up the hill he noticed a black car following them. A lot of cars were black, but he could tell it was one of the black cars that had brought the gangs to Tibbetts Park. He just couldn't tell which gang it belonged to.

"Don't look back," he told Amira. "Look in the side-view mirror and tell me what you see."

"I see a black car following us."

"Yeah, that's what I see."

"Why are they following us?"

"Because they don't want us to tell the police what happened last night."

"Then we better get there before they stop us."

As they approached the hospital the light was green, so they didn't have to stop. The next light was red, and he decided to run it. But looking ahead toward the intersection at Roberts Avenue, he saw another black car blocking their way. If he kept going, they would be trapped between the two black cars. The only way out was to make a quick U-turn and head back the other way and go to Hastings.

"Where are we going?" Amira asked, swaying with the turn.

"We're going to the Hastings police station."

He stepped on the accelerator and went up the hill. The next two lights were green, but he had to run the lights at Odell Terrace and Executive Boulevard. As they sped toward Hastings a black car was tailgating them and bumping into them. Another black car was trying to pull even with them and force them off the road.

At that point he had no choice but to floor the accelerator and try to outrun the black cars.

They were going at top speed when a moving van suddenly emerged from Tompkins Avenue without stopping and turned onto Broadway, blocking the entire road.

He slammed on the brakes and leaned over to protect Amira. The car behind them rammed them and drove them into the moving van.

From the newspaper Sister Maura learned that a car with two students from St. Catherine had crashed into a moving van on Broadway, a car that was following them had crashed into them, and another car had gone off the road and crashed into a tree. The people in the front seats of all three cars were killed, and the people in the back seats of two cars were seriously injured.

Based on what Milos and Amira had told her, Sister Maura developed a theory about what had caused the accident. She shared her theory with the Hastings police detective who was handling the case. His name was John Murphy, and he was a graduate of the criminal justice program at St. Catherine. He had been a student in her ethics and religion courses.

They met in her office a few days after the accident. John was sitting in front of her desk where he sat as a student years ago. He was heavier now, and his brown hair was flecked with gray, but he had the same look of tough intelligence in his eyes.

After going through the preliminaries with him she said: "The newspaper said that the people in two of the cars were alleged gang members."

"They were definitely gang members," John said. "One of the gangs was from the Bronx, and the other was from Yonkers."

"Well, I knew the two students in the car that crashed into the moving van."

John took out a notebook, thumbed through it, and read: "Milos Stojanovic and Amira Hasanic."

"They were both in my religion class, and they were both in Tibbetts Park when their cousins were killed."

"You mean Bojan Stojanovic and Hasan Hasanic?"

"Bojan was Milos's cousin, and Hasan was Amira's cousin. Bojan was a Serb and Hasan was a Bosniak. Their families were refugees from the war in Bosnia."

John frowned. "From what the Yonkers police told me, it looks like they continued their war in America."

"They did, and they brought gangs into their war. It escalated from vandalism to destruction of family businesses. Milos and Amira were trying to make peace, so they got their cousins to ask the two gangs to meet in Tibbetts Park to talk about ending the war. A few gang members were wounded in that war, and the gang leaders wanted blood from the cousins in payment for the blood of their members. When they met that night the gang leaders gave the cousins knives and made them fight each other. One gang leader pushed Hasan, who was holding a knife, into Bojan and killed him. When Milos picked up Bojan's knife so no one else could use it, the other gang leader grabbed his hand and pushed it into Hasan and killed him. So the gang leaders did the killing."

"There are two sets of prints on the knife that killed Hasan," John said. "One set was Milos's and the other set was Bojan's. So if one of the gang leaders used that knife to kill Hasan, why aren't his prints on it?"

"He didn't hold the knife. As I just told you, he grabbed Milos's hand that was holding the knife and pushed it into Hasan."

John looked doubtful. "How do you know what happened?"

"I have reliable witnesses."

"Milos and Amira?"

"They came to the college and met with me the next morning, and they told me what happened."

"And you believed them?"

"Of course I believed them. They were good kids."

John was silent for a while, evidently accepting her judgment, and then he asked. "So where were they going when they had the accident?"

"They were going to tell the police what happened."

"They were driving north, so they weren't going to the station on Shonnard Place."

"They said they were going to Shonnard Place, but they must have run into the cars of the gangs and turned around and headed for the Hastings station."

"That makes sense. From what we found at the scene of the accident, there were two cars pursuing them. One of them tried to run them off the road, and the other one rammed them as the driver slammed on the brakes to avoid crashing into the van. Since the gang leaders were in the front seats of their cars, they were both killed."

"May God have mercy on them."

John sighed. "I know we were crazy when we were that age, but this is way beyond crazy. I feel bad for the families of your students."

"I do too. I also feel bad for the families of the gang leaders."

"Yeah, the families always pay for what their children do." He put away his notebook and rose from the chair. "Well, thanks, sister. Thanks for helping me solve this case, and thanks for teaching me ethics and religion."

"I hope you got something out of my courses."

"I did," he said. "What I got from them helps me deal with these situations."

Several days later she met with the families of Milos and Amira. Since there were thirteen of them she reserved the conference room in Morrissey Hall to accommodate them all.

As they sat down around the table with Milos's family on one side and Amira's family on the other, she could feel the hostility between them. Evidently, each family blamed the other for their children's deaths.

"Thank you for coming," Sister Maura said, sitting at the head of the table. "Why don't we introduce ourselves, going clockwise around the table. I'm Maura, a Religious Sister of the Redemption. I teach at the college."

"I'm Goran," the man to her left said. "I'm Bojan's father and Milos's uncle."

They went around the table, fathers and mothers and sons and daughters and the grandmother, ending with the man to her right, who said: "I'm Ahmed. I'm Hasan's father and Amira's uncle."

"Thank you," she said. "I'm so sorry for your losses. There's nothing worse than losing children."

No one moved, and no one said a word.

"I want to help you understand what happened to your children. Your sons," she said, addressing the parents of Bojan and Hassan, "were at war with each other, and they brought gangs into their war. Bojan's gang was from Yonkers, and Hasan's gang was from the Bronx. At some point the gangs took over, and the war got out of control."

"*Šta je rekla?*" the grandmother asked.

Goran translated for her.

"Milos and Amira met in my religion class, and they fell in love before he knew she was a Bosniak and before she knew he was a Serb. Their being from different religions didn't matter to them. And when they saw the war between Bojan and Hasan, they tried to make peace. But the war escalated, and by the time the gangs met in Tibbetts Park a few of their members had been wounded, so the leaders wanted blood from Bojan and Hassan. They gave Bojan and Hasan knives to fight each other. And though Milos and Amira tried to stop them, the gang leaders got their blood from Bojan and Hasan."

"The police said the gang leaders killed them," Goran said.

"Milos and Amira witnessed it, and they were going to the police in Hastings to tell them what happened. But the gang leaders wanted to stop them from going to the police, so they chased them in their cars, and they caused the accident."

"What happened to the gang leaders?"

"They were killed too."

"So they won't be prosecuted?"

"They're beyond being prosecuted here on this earth."

"But that's not justice," Goran said.

"We shouldn't want justice," Malika said. "That's what they wanted in Bosnia, and look what happened."

"That's what our sons wanted," Vidra said, "and look what happened."

Goran considered. "Well, if we shouldn't want justice, then what should we want?"

"You should want what Milos and Amira wanted," Sister Maura said.

"And what did they want?"

"They wanted peace."

"The sister's right," Malika said. "We came here to get away from war. I don't want what happened to our children to happen to anyone else's children."

"I don't either," Vidra said.

"Then let's make peace," Malika said, offering her hand.

Vidra reached across the table and clasped it.

Following the example of their wives, Goran and Ahmed reached across the table and clasped hands. The children followed the example of their parents. And finally the woman with the sweet blue eyes who looked like Milos reached across the table to the man with the soulful dark eyes who looked like Amira, and they clasped hands.

"To honor Milos and Amira as peacemakers," Sister Maura told them, "I'm raising money for a statue. I have the president's approval to install it on the campus."

"*Šta je rekla?*" the grandmother asked.

Goran translated for her.

"I know you're still recovering from the destruction of your businesses, but I'm asking you to donate something now as a token of your commitment to peace."

"How much would be appropriate?" Goran asked.

"If each family donated a hundred dollars, it would signify your good faith."

Before either of the fathers could get out their wallets, the two uncles each produced bills and handed them to her.

"Thank you. I don't have to tell you how special Milos and Amira were. They wanted more than anything to make peace between their families. In fact, they died for it. So I hope they'll finally get what they wanted."

"Speaking for our family," Goran said, "I can say they will."

"I can say they will," Ahmed said. "But they shouldn't have had to assume that responsibility. We should have assumed it. I'm sorry, princess."

"Your mother in heaven is very proud of you," Malika said with tears in her eyes.

A year later they all came to the inauguration of the statue. By then the students had planted a ring of birch trees in a peace garden in front of Wagner Hall to commemorate the attack on September 11, and the statue was placed in the middle of them.

Along with the students and faculty and staff who attended the ceremony, the two families mingled easily, as if they had gotten together since the meeting in the conference room. Milos's mother and Amira's father were having a conversation in Bosnian, while the younger brothers of Bojan and Hasan were talking with each other in English.

It was a clear, sunny day, as it had been a year ago when the hijacked planes flew into the towers. By now the air over the city was clear of the foul dust that had lingered for months and blurred the skyline.

When the bronze statue was unveiled you saw a girl wearing a headscarf and a boy with a cross around his neck. They were holding hands and gazing hopefully into the future.

Threading her way through the family members, Sister Maura moved closer to the statue to make sure the inscription on the base was correct. It said:

Milos and Amira
1983 – 2001
Children of God

BOOK CLUB GUIDE

Milos and Amira

Tom Milton

Introduction

Milos and Amira are refugees from the war in Bosnia. Milos is a Serb, a Christian, and his family suffered losses from acts of violence committed against them by Bosniaks, the major ethnic group in their city. After losing his uncle in the war he was able to escape with his family and come to America. Amira is a Bosniak, a Muslim, and her family suffered losses from acts of violence committed against them by Serbs. After losing her mother in the war she was able to escape with her family and come to America. Five years later they are living in Yonkers with their families, and they have just begun their freshman year at St. Catherine College when terrorists destroy the World Trade Center. Since the terrorists were presumptive Muslims there is a strong anti-Muslim feeling in their community, and after being attacked verbally while wearing her headscarf in public Amira stops wearing it at the college. When she appears without a headscarf in the religion class that they are both taking, she inadvertently reveals to Milos the most beautiful girl he has ever seen. When the professor, Sister Maura, invites students to talk about the attack, a few of them blame Muslims, but Milos argues that the men who flew the planes into the towers were not motivated by their religion but only by hate, and that if there had been any love in their hearts they wouldn't have done it. That gets Amira's attention, and drawn together, they fall in love.

Milos lives with his father and mother and two sisters on the upper floor of a two-family house in an urban neighborhood of Yonkers. The house is owned by his Uncle Goran, his father's brother, who got out of Yugoslavia ten years before it disintegrated. Milos's family remained in Yugoslavia, in their hometown of Zenica, until Bosniaks destroyed his father's auto repair shop and killed his mother's brother. When his family arrived as refugees from the war, Goran gave his brother a job at his auto repair shop in Yonkers and made the upper half of his house available for his brother's family. Though Milos didn't know a word of English when he came to America at the age of thirteen, he adapted to his new country and graduated from high school with a good enough average to be accepted into the physical therapy program at St. Catherine College.

Amira lives with her father and her younger brother on the lower floor of a two-family house in another urban neighborhood of Yonkers. The house is owned by her Uncle Ahmed, her father's brother, who got out of Yugoslavia more than ten years before it disintegrated. Amira's family remained in Yugoslavia, in their hometown of Srebrenica, until it was taken over by Serbs. Among the thousands of Bosniaks who perished in the siege of that city, her mother was abducted and killed. When her family arrived as refugees from the war, Ahmed gave his brother a job in the kitchen of his deli in downtown Yonkers, and Amira was taken under the wing of her Aunt Malika, her mother's sister, who has raised her in the strict traditions of their religion. Though Amira didn't know a word of English when she came to America at the age of thirteen, she graduated from high school with straight A's and was accepted into the social work program at St. Catherine College.

While their families have reasons for being hostile to each other, they came to America with the hope of leaving the war behind them and living in peace. But the war resumes with an act of aggression by Bojan, a cousin of Milos who gets caught up in the anti-Muslim feeling aroused by the attack on the World Trade Center. Bojan goes to Ahmed's deli, and he sprays a message on the window, saying: "Muslims, go home." He has a bumper stick on his truck with the same message, so when Milos hears about the message sprayed on the window he suspects that Bojan was the perpetrator, and he tries to persuade Bojan to stop committing such acts of hatred because they are morally wrong. Meanwhile, Hasan, a cousin of Amira, enlists some guys from a gang in the Bronx to watch the store at night and prevent further acts of vandalism. Determined to pursue his mission, Bojan goes back to the store at night to spray his message on the window again, and the guys who are watching store not only stop him but also break his arm. Milos pleads with Bojan not to get even, but Bojan goes back to the store with some guys he has enlisted from a gang in Yonkers and breaks the window of the store. Amira pleads with Hasan not to get even, but Hasan goes with his guys to the house where Bojan lives with his family and breaks the window of his beloved truck and carves a message on its hood, saying: "Serbs, go home." Trying to make peace, Milos and Amira ask Sister Maura to act as a neutral referee in a meeting between Bojan and Hasan, which might bring them to their senses, but by then the war, having escalated into a gang war, is out of control.

A conversation with Tom Milton

In this novel I found the themes of war and peace that occur in your previous novels, but your treatment of them is different here. For one thing, this novel reads like a play, and of course it was based on a play, the one about the star-crossed lovers.

It's a retelling of Romeo and Juliet, as was one of my favorite musicals, Westside Story. It's been in my head for a long time, and I finally found a setting for it—a community with refugees from the war in Bosnia who thought they had escaped from ethnic conflict by coming to America.

As I understand it, though the ethnic groups in that war shared a language and other features of their cultures, the thing that divided them was religion, with Serbs being Eastern Orthodox, Croats being Roman Catholic, and Bosniaks being Muslim.

I spent some time there during the year before they went to war, and from what I could see, religion was the main thing that divided them.

The characters in your story are Serbs and Bosniaks who settled in the city of Yonkers. Were these characters based on people you knew?

No. But I had students from those groups, so I got to know a little about them.

The boy in your story, Milos, is a Serb, and the girl, Amira, is a Bosniak. They meet in a class at St. Catherine College, a setting in many of your novels.

A lot of my characters have some connection with the college. In fact, it serves as a home base of my fictional world.

Your story begins a few days after the attack on the World Trade Center, which arouses anti-Muslim feelings in the community. Amira, a devout Muslim, is afraid to wear her headscarf in public. Did you see that reaction to the attack?

Oh, yes. I had a secretary who was a Muslim, and after the attack her family disappeared for two weeks and went into hiding, they were so afraid of being persecuted.

When Amira comes to class without her headscarf she reveals herself as a beautiful young woman, and Milos falls in love with her. And when he says in a class discussion that the men who flew the planes into the towers weren't motivated by their religion but only by hate, he reveals himself as a nice young man, and Amira falls in love with him.

Like the boy and girl in the other versions of this story, they fall in love at first sight.

But they're also different from the boy and girl in the other versions. I mean, one thing that makes them different is that both of them are seriously religious.

Yes, they are. And though the conflict between their ethnic groups is rooted in their different religions, their faith in God is a source of the love between them. From their prayers it's clear that they both believe in a merciful and forgiving God, so religion doesn't divide them, it brings them together and raises their love to a higher level.

I noticed that they meet in a college religion course, where they learn from the professor, Sister Maura, that whatever their religion, people of faith all believe in the same God.

You may have also noticed that it's Amira who shows Milos the statue of the Virgin Mary on the campus, and he learns from her that Mary has a whole chapter of the Quran devoted to her.

So the love that Milos and Amira have for each other goes beyond the physical attraction of a teenage crush.

It becomes transcendent. It ultimately becomes a force for peace.

Well, let's go back to the theme of war. At one level I think you've written a fable about war, which gets to the heart of war and its causes.

It starts when a group or a country does something violent to another group or country, and then that group or country does something violent to get even, and driven by the insatiable urge to get even, it escalates until the violence gets out of control.

In your story the war starts with Bojan and Hasan, who are cousins of Milos and Amira. Unlike the other members of their families, these two guys are inflamed with ethnic hatred. Why didn't they learn from what happened in Bosnia?

They didn't experience the war, so they don't know what it's like. They're typical of many Americans, who don't know what war is like because they haven't experienced it.

From your personal history, I know that you've experienced war.

Too many times, in too many places.

Bojan and Hasan get into a war with each other with minor acts of vandalism, and it escalates into a major conflict.

The mechanism that escalates their war is the need for each of them to get even with the other. And that's why wars are so hard to stop. If both parties don't feel that enough is enough, then they keep wanting to get even.

Bojan and Hasan bring gangs into their war, just as countries bring outside powers into their wars.

That's happened in most of the wars of the past two centuries. And when you bring outside powers into your war, you lose control. It's no longer your war but their war.

The war between Bojan and Hasan occurs within the context of the wider war between America and terrorists, who in the minds of too many Americans and their political leaders are identified with Muslims. So both wars are in a sense wars of religion.

They are, but let's remember what Milos says in class when we first meet him, that the men who flew the planes into the towers weren't motivated by their religion but only by hate. And hate can be aroused by any perceived difference between one group and another group. So in any ostensible war of religion, the difference in religion is only a pretext. When people are filled with hate, they can find any pretext for a war.

In addition to their ethnic conflict Bojan and Hasan have personal reasons for their war, especially Hasan, who lusts for his cousin Amira and is jealous of any boy with whom she has a relationship. So her boyfriend being a Serb intensifies his hatred for Serbs.

Ironically, while Milos and Amira believe that their relationship is a reason for peace between their families, their cousins make it a pretext for war, and Milos and Amira end up feeling responsible for it.

Let's talk about Sister Maura, who has played a role in All the Flowers, The Silver Locket, *and* The Lost Summer. *The story begins and ends with her point of view, while in the middle it alternates between the points of view of the lovers. I assume that one of your purposes is to give us an adult perspective.*

That's right. She also provides a religious perspective, which she does in her religion course. She introduces the theme that whatever our religion, we're children of God. And she frames the story.

Going back to what I said in the beginning, it reads like a play, and like the other versions of the story, it races ahead with the impetuousness of young people. But Sister Maura provides some pauses for reflection.

That's intended. Things move so fast, as they often do in life. By the time you realize what's happening, it's already happened.

I think it's appropriate that the story ends with Sister Maura's point of view. Your main theme reverberates with her.

That's why I wrote this novel, not only to give people a good story with a pair of sympathetic characters but also to give them the feeling that I hope you got when you read the last page.

Discussion questions

1. This novel is a version of the Romeo and Juliet story. What features does it have in common with other versions of this story?

2. How is it different from other versions of this story?

3. Why is it significant that Milos and Amira meet in a religion class? How is their religion class used to elucidate the novel's themes?

4. How did the attack on the World Center set in motion both the love between Milos and Amira and the hate between Bojan and Hasan?

5. Describe what you think were the formative influences on Milos and Amira, and explain why they are so different from Bojan and Hasan.

6. What are the causes of the war between Bojan and Hasan?

7. Did Bojan and Hasan bring their ethnic hatred with them from Bosnia, or did they acquire it in America?

8. How did their bringing gangs into their war fit the pattern of regional wars and civil wars over the past two centuries?

9. How does the war between their cousins affect the relationship between Milos and Amira?

10. What methods did Milos and Amira employ as peacemakers?

11. Why were they unable to stop the war between Bojan and Hasan before it got out of control?

12. Why were Goran and Ahmed ineffective at controlling the behavior of their sons?

13. In what sense is this novel a fable of war?

14. Explain the role of Sister Maura in the story.

15. Explain the roles of Pamet and Rafid, the younger brothers of Bojan and Hasan.

16. Does the ending resolve the issues of the conflict between the families of Milos and Amira?

www.ingramcontent.com/pod-product-compliance
Lightning Source LLC
LaVergne TN
LVHW012009260326
834688LV00057B/339